Moroccan Dreams

Moroccan Dreams

PART ONE

DAVINA CALBRAITH

T

Troubador Publishing Ltd
Unit E2 Airfield Business Park,
Harrison Road, Market Harborough,
Leicestershire LE16 7UL
Tel: 0116 279 2299
Email: books@troubador.co.uk
Web: www.troubador.co.uk

ISBN 978 1 83628 233 4

British Library Cataloguing in Publication Data.
A catalogue record for this book is available from the British Library.

The manufacturer's authorised representative in the EU for product safety is Authorised Rep Compliance Ltd, 71 Lower Baggot Street, Dublin D02 P593 Ireland (www.arccompliance.com).

Printed and bound in Great Britain by 4edge Limited
Typeset in 11pt Minion Pro by Troubador Publishing Ltd, Leicester, UK

Dedicated to all hard-working souls
whose efforts are not appreciated

Chapter 1

Wrong Choices

Suzie Watson sat with her mouth hanging open in stunned silence. She hastily closed it again when she remembered she was slap bang in the middle of an airport, about to fly off to start the adventure of a lifetime.

When she thought back to a month ago there had been nothing remarkable about that particular Sunday. It had been the usual routine. She had sat with arms folded across her chest, leaning on her sister's spotless kitchen island with her head drooped, whilst her sister droned on relentlessly about how 'weak' Suzie was. Suzie screwed up her mouth and clenched her fists but said nothing as her sister filled a fine bone China mug from the kettle and set it down in front of her. This kitchen was nothing like hers. Granted it was pristine and expensive, but it had no soul.

"Are you listening?" her sister had demanded.

"Yes... I..."

1

"'Cos if you're not listening, I'm wasting my breath."

"Go on then." Suzie sighed. And boy did she go on. It was no use saying anything though. As usual, Suzie was way past arguing. Her sister spent most of her time being sullen and negative. The only time this was not true was when she would chew people's heads off during frenzied bursts of aggression. The rest of the time she just didn't bother talking to Suzie at all. Sisterly love. It was like being related to a piranha.

The next day at work at the advertising agency had passed quickly. Suzie had made her way to the boardroom and found that she was the first one there. Not that this mattered, nobody seemed to notice her brilliant timekeeping. She had tried to become more 'visible' in meetings lately, as she always felt like she was 'standing alone on the sand with the tide going out'. True, she had a good rapport with colleagues but never felt truly confident. As the meeting got underway, the usual preamble of previous minutes was dealt with and the debate on issues began.

"I definitely think we should head towards 'healthy-living ads' for this brand," Charlie said.

"That would go down well with young mums too," Ian interjected.

A brief silence. Now was Suzie's chance. The sea was lapping at her feet. She went for it. "I think—"

"Definitely needs a better strapline though," Isabel said.

Suzie tried again. "How about—"

More voices joined the fray. "Yes, definitely a new strapline. This one sounds like a wet blanket. We need something with more va-va-voom."

Suzie's heart beat quickly. She was now eager to speak as she had the answer. "What about-"

"A blue sports car with the words 'Drive it like you stole it' underneath is what it needs!" Isabel finished. A large chorus of 'Yeah!' and a spontaneous burst of back-slapping broke out amongst the others.

Suzie had started to wonder whether she was actually still there, dreaming, or magically transported to some parallel universe. She said nothing. They all left to head for a celebratory drink at the bar next door with Isabel, her best friend, leaving Suzie alone once more. So much for not letting the tide go out. It had gone out so far she couldn't even see the sea now.

Isabel in particular was always better than her, better at knowing exactly what to say and do in any situation. On the long walk back to her office she had stopped off to check e-mails and pick up the late post before heading off home. There was only one e-mail which had not been there before the board meeting. It was from her line manager:

You are being moved to the Marrakesh office. You will be given one month to decide whether you want to take up this kind offer permanently. I suggest you start thinking about this and we will talk tomorrow.

Just that. No warning, no reason given, no description of the new job, and nothing that told her why this was happening. Great! It had been the perfect end to a perfect day.

So here she was now, a month later, waiting for her best friend Isabel and watching the flight board for her flight number to come up. Threatening storm clouds had gathered on the horizon before Suzie had entered the airport building, in a solid blanket of grey, the drizzle was unending.

Suzie remembered that streams of water had run down the steamy bus windows as her flat came into view that day four weeks ago too, the day she had received news of her new Moroccan job. By 7pm on that day, Suzie had been knee-deep in clothes washing and washing-up from the night before. Simultaneously, she had been trying to flip sausages in a frying pan. Suzie always cooked whatever was to hand, unlike her sister. Her sister didn't have fridge magnets like normal people, instead she had a ten-point plan featuring the whole months' meals but would then suddenly go 'off piste' and cook what she liked for no apparent reason. What was the point of that?

Suzie took a deep breath and sighed as she recalled the conversation with her boyfriend. "I got completely trounced in the boardroom today."

Her boyfriend had lolled against the arm of the sofa with his eyes glued to his phone screen. 'Huh?' came the reply.

"I was totally trampled underfoot actually..."

"That's nice..." He looked up momentarily as he put his feet up on the sofa and swiped his phone screen.

Suzie continued. "Then I got chased by a dragon and eaten by goblins... after being covered with chili sauce..."

Silence.

She should have known better than to expect any kind of emotional support from him. He had the emotional intelligence of a gnat at the best of times and had not even seen (let alone understood) what the problem was when their love life had stalled completely last month.

"I'm moving to Morocco at the end of the month…" she continued. Still no response. Okay then. She would bloomin' well say yes to her boss tomorrow, but first she had to tell her mum.

Without a word, she had put on her scarf and coat and slid silently out the front door. Suzie had arrived wet and dripping all over Mum's floor. Her mum had looked disdainfully at Suzie as she held out her coat, and eyed the growing puddle on the floor wondering how long it would take to mop it up.

"There you go," her mum said as handed Suzie a steaming cup of coffee. "You look tired. Are they working you too hard, Suzanne?"

Suzie had taken the cup and curled up in the comfy armchair by the fire and had told her mum about the proposal to send her to Morocco, how she felt about it, and her boyfriend's indifference.

"Oh, love…" her mum said with feeling. So much feeling in fact that Suzie thought she was actually about to say something nice. Something along the lines of how she would miss her. "Oh, love…" Mum continued. "Do they know how bad you are at sales and photography?" Just at that moment Suzie's sister had let herself in through the door and Suzie struggled to rearrange her stunned face. Had her sister caught that last remark?

Her sister smiled. Never a good sign. "Yes, Suzie… don't you remember when we asked you to take a picture of us on that ferry and you fell backwards and nearly fell off the edge? And what about that time you tried to sell peanuts at the church bazaar? And what about t—"

"That's not the point!" Suzie screamed. "This has

5

nothing to do with photography! Or sales... At least I don't think it has..."

"No... you're right, love." Mum patted Suzie's knee. "*Even* your boyfriend won't want you to go. It's more about you always making wrong choices for your life..."

"*What*? What do you mean?"

"I said wrong choices... No... Don't take this Morocco thing. Stay here and for once in your life make the right choice."

Suzie exhaled. That settled it. She was going. There was nothing to stop her now. Mum always did have a way with words.

Suzie's thoughts floated onto today's events. She had arrived at the airport this morning ridiculously early, but then she always did. She had inspected all the airport shops, sighed at the prices, bought nothing, and then returned to where Isabel would be joining her. She had tilted her head this way and that, hoping to catch sight of her. Over the last few months she had often had to collect Isabel's train tickets when they went anywhere. Well, if Isabel was late she would have to check in herself this time!

Suzie scanned the constant stream of people milling past – tall people, short people, bald people, people with pushchairs, and oversized cases. Stopping to glance a little longer at a lean-legged woman who wasn't Isabel, she sighed out loud. Where had she got to this time? As if Suzie didn't know. Isabel's life was so full, so busy. Not like hers. Suzie had no fun, and up to now no future... dull family, dull colleagues, empty fridge, empty flat most of the time. In fact, empty life. But not for much longer! If she stayed in the UK she knew she would not be promoted anytime soon as there were too many people waiting to 'cut you down at the knees' given half a chance, but she was sure everything would be different in Morocco.

Suzie sat listening to the rain as it beat out a continuous and hypnotic rhythm on the departure lounge roof. Not a good evening to fly. Rooting through her bag for something comforting, her hand fell upon something crinkly to the touch. Ah, one of the Belgian chocolates that Isabel had bought her for her birthday! The golden wrapper promised something sweet and delicious – something with 'melt-in-the-mouth gorgeousness'. But as Suzie popped the chocolate into her mouth, this, like most of Isabel's presents if she was honest, was all a little disappointing. Shame. Isabel seemed to have spent so much time choosing them. This present apparently took three whole lunch hours, which for Isabel, was a lot.

Suzie always longed to be confident and articulate in the boardroom like Isabel, but somehow someone else always got in there first and it was always with the point she wanted to make. In Morocco all this would change. She would make this a brand-new start. After all, it couldn't be worse than the humdrum life she had been leading. For a brief moment a smile crept over her face as she thought about how her family would welcome back a new confident person. They would see her with fresh eyes. Just as quickly the smile was completely erased from her face, in much the same way as marker pen writing can be erased on a whiteboard. 'Reckless' her boyfriend had called her. *Well, if this is reckless, it feels damn good.* Was she afraid that he would get cross? Did she feel guilty about telling him that it was only for four weeks? The answer was no. Despite her attempts to calm the situation, a heated argument had ensued in the last week and she had not seen him since. He knew she was leaving today but she had not heard from him, despite her copious unanswered phone messages.

Isabel arrived just as the flight number flicked upwards. The two quickly made their way to the café and ordered breakfast. Suzie watched Isabel cut up her piece of bacon with a worrying amount of precision, just like watching a surgeon at work. The one saving grace in all this was the fact that Isabel, her best friend at the advertising agency, had received the same e-mail from the boss that day with the same offer to send them to Morocco.

Isabel finished the last bit of her egg as their boarding number appeared. Suzie did a last check of her luggage as they got up to start this exciting new chapter in their lives. They looked at each other, hugged, and grinned.

"Come on," Isabel said. "Together we can take on the world. Girl power! Get ready Morocco, because here we come!"

Chapter 2

Flying High

Once up in the air it was the usual mixture of prepacked food and expensive duty-free. Isabel ordered her obligatory G and T, expertly repaired a broken nail, and now sat snoozing. Finding a place to live had been easy, as the Moroccan side of the ad agency company had a flat they leased to employees that needed somewhere after relocating. It was currently vacant and had been told they were free to live there indefinitely. As Isabel was snoozing it gave Suzie the opportunity to plan how she would make the ad agency's small flat into a home. Suzie leafed through the photographs the agency had sent her, and several sketches and lists later she knew exactly what she needed to buy from the souks when she landed. She couldn't wait.

Her thoughts about the last month drifted here and there, like the wispy clouds she could see through the plane windows. Suzie thought about the way she had marched into her line manager's office and told him she was fine with his decision to send her to Morocco.

He had looked surprised at her sudden decisiveness but said nothing. They had a short perfunctory chat about plane tickets, living accommodation, and the Marrakesh office, and the deed was done. At this point she was unaware that Isabel had got the same offer and went to find her. She felt sure that Isabel would need a stiff drink when she told her, as she and Suzie had become good friends over a very short period of time. She had found Isabel looking uncharacteristically studious at her computer.

"Got five minutes? I have some new accounts I would like you to see," Suzie said. This was their code for 'let's get out of here and get a coffee'.

"Yes, of course," Isabel had replied. "I can always make time for you." Five minutes later, with cappuccino in hand, she handed Isabel the sugar and told her of the plan to send her to Morocco. "Oh... *that*..." Isabel laughed. "Bit of a promotion, I reckon. They have obviously seen our potential. I'm going to Morocco too!"

"Oh wow! He didn't tell me anyone else was going! Both of us together..." Suzie thought for a moment. "That will be great! Great parties, great girlie shopping trips... I can't wait now! Oh, Isabel, I am so pleased!" Suzie hugged her with joy.

During the days that had followed this conversation, Suzie's boyfriend got more and more sulky and unsociable. He swore blind that Suzie had not told him about Morocco, and then when she ignored his constant bleating he accused her of ignoring how he felt. She remembered when she had first met him – he had saved her from countless attacks from the local office bully by wading in and sticking up for her. She had always admired him for that as it more than made up for the areas he was lacking in. Although lately she was not so sure. There had been no trace of this admirable quality in him over the last few months. He just seemed to want to stop her doing anything that was enjoyable. Morocco was a case in point. On the other hand, even her family seemed to like him which was a miracle in itself.

"Look… I don't know what the problem is," Suzie lied to keep the peace. "It's only for a month, then I will be back."

"Only a month?"

"Yes… I am sure you will survive. You seemed to survive okay on your own on the cricket tour you took for five weeks." Gotcha! He couldn't argue with that.

"Well… If it is only for a month, I guess it's okay. If that's what you want."

"Yes. I have made up my mind."

"Heard that before."

"This time it's different."

"Heard that before too."

"This time it will be."

*

A week before Suzie was due to leave, she had gone to her Aunt Saffy and Uncle Tom's Silver Wedding Anniversary party and the whole family had been invited. Uncle Tom had been the life and soul of the party until Mum told him about Suzie's shock departure to Morocco.

"You're not really going, are you?" Uncle Tom had said.

"Yes, afraid so, Uncle."

"But what about your man?"

"He's staying here." Seeing her uncle's doubtful look, Suzie added, "I'm definitely going as it may be the best offer I get for a long time. I am determined it will work out for the good."

"We've all heard that before, darling," Suzie's mum said, frowning.

"Yeah, I said that" Suzie's boyfriend added and scowled at her.

Annoyed at their total lack of support, Suzie got up to get a refill, but as she wandered over to the bar she overheard her cousin talking to Aunt Saffy.

"Of course she won't really go. I know she says that, but really? Suzie? Going to Morocco? Can you actually see her making a go of it?"

Suzie would show them. She would show the whole bloomin' lot of them this time!

The last week in the UK had been a flurry of activity – visa, money exchange, travel insurance, and finishing up all the UK work so that anyone covering would find everything in good order. A couple of days before 'lift-off' she had received an e-mail to confirm the Moroccan flat had been cleaned and was ready for its two new occupants and Christine, a long-time friend of Suzie's, had of course wanted to know every exciting detail and had insisted on taking Suzie for a celebratory drink when she had heard the news.

"So… what's the boyfriend's view?" Christine had asked.

"Better. At least he's talking to me now. But he's telling everyone I won't go."

"Ha! He'll get a shock then! Come on, I want to take you somewhere. I think you'll like it." Christine led her to the back of a pub she had never seen before and up some stairs.

"Are we supposed to be back here?" Suzie gasped.

"Come on. Close your eyes…" Christine took her by the hand, then placed her free hand over Suzie's eyes. "And open them!" They were now standing at the entrance to a very swish lounge decorated with rich deep colours. Velvet red curtains graced the windows, flock wallpaper covered the walls, and brass filigree lightshades stood at various point across the room. It definitely looked full of 'Eastern promise'. Suzie had no idea this was even here.

"I thought a Moroccan-themed wine bar would be just the ticket," explained Christine. The rest of the night had been an alcohol-induced blur, ending in exotic Moroccan-themed cocktails. "So…" Christine said dramatically with wild hand gestures. "What are you going to do with boyfriend? You can't commute to Morocco you know, it's too far."

"I'm going."

"Yes, but what will he do?"

"Don't know."

"What about your flat here?"

"I really don't know, Christine. I'll sort it, but I am definitely going."

"Good for you!" Christine hiccoughed and fell off the stool. "Good for you, buddy. Cheers!"

Suzie's thoughts drifted back to the present. She only had one question left. It was clear why the office had chosen

Isabel, but why would they choose someone like Suzie with her lack of ability in the boardroom and sales to be the one to jet off to Morocco? She shuddered momentarily, trying to shake off the negative thought. The overhead lights in the plane flickered on, indicating they were due to land soon. She reached for her seatbelt. "Buckle up, Suzie girl, today is the first day of the rest of your life."

Chapter 3

Arriving in Marrakesh

A wall of heat hit them as they clambered down the plane steps. Suzie thought at first it was something to do with the plane engines but when it did not subside she realised this was the actual temperature. Man, it was hot!

At arrivals they were met by a friendly guy holding out a placard with the ad agency name on it, who ushered them into his taxi. They were obviously expected and it boded well that the company had seen fit to lay on transport for them. She had never been picked up by a man with a placard before! As they relaxed into the leather seats, the taxi sped past a mixture of new and then older-looking buildings and a series of minarets. The ride was short, and mercifully it had air conditioning. The man gave them a set of keys to the company flat in a brown envelope and sent them on their way.

The flat was not quite as the picture had shown. Although a little welcome basket with basic supplies had been placed in the kitchen, it was clear that the photographs had been taken when it was first new. Judging by the worn carpet, scratched kitchen units, and stained toilet, this was now ten years on. Not surprisingly, it was not up to Isabel's usual standards and she complained bitterly, but other than these faults it was clean enough. No different to Suzie's flat back in the UK really.

After a brief walk to 'clear her head', Isabel announced that she was going to lie down, so Suzie set off to find the nearest medina for proper supplies. However, the men behind the stalls appeared to be either too pushy or too busy to serve her. They became strangely engrossed in straightening rows of bags, smoothing down carpets, or swatting flies as she passed. The only guy that had actually spoken to her directly seemed inexplicably to be having a real go at her because she didn't want to buy anything he had for sale. Suzie made a mental note to avoid that stall in the future and buy any stuff she needed elsewhere. Twenty minutes later, she was almost back at the flat with no supplies to show for her outing. She was so frustrated that she stood with her hand against her face just staring into space.

"Excuse me…" a voice said behind her. "Are you Suzie or Isabel?" She swung around where a young man of twenty or so dressed in jeans stood looking at her. She figured no-one else would have randomly put those two names together unless they knew of her, so she nodded. He was obviously British too judging by the accent. "Sorry, I should introduce myself. I'm Tony from the ad agency. They told me to expect Suzie and Isabel today and asked me to come and take you both around as part of the welcome here, did they not mention this?"

Suzie found her voice: "Hi, yes, I'm Suzie. Nice to meet you." She shook his hand. "No, they didn't mention it."

"Isabel not here?" he enquired.

"No, she's sleeping."

"Did you find the supplies basket I left in the flat?"

"Oh, that was you? Yes, thank you."

"Just a few basics to get you started." He followed her gaze. "I see you have already seen the medina across from the flat. Locals call them souks. Sorry, I was running a little late. Meant to be here a little earlier. By the way, the locals here just think that you are a tourist if you are white, female, and in European dress. Marrakesh is a lot more European than it used to be but there are still some stallholders here who aren't. You will find the younger guys a lot more amenable in the quarter across town."

"That explains a lot. About the stallholders I mean."

"Follow me," he said. "I will take you to the *real* souks." She did as she was asked. He seemed pleasant enough as they chatted about her journey and how different life was here in Morocco.

The first thing that hit Suzie as they entered the souk was the vast array of rich colours. Pinks, plums, golds, oranges, greens and blues of every shade. Assorted smells of cooking mingled with the pungent smell of spices where countless pointed mounds of vibrantly coloured spices were piled high with hues of reds, browns, yellows and oranges. This gave way to rows and rows of bags, scarves, and carpets as far as the eye could see. People bustled this way and that, and the chatter was constant. It felt so alive. This was a real assault on the senses! She loved it! It was like her eyes were in withdrawal, they were hungry and just couldn't get enough.

On the way back to the flat with arms full of goodies, Suzie noticed for the first time that the streets beyond this souk gave way to dishevelled buildings, peeling paint, and rickety wooden doors. These had obviously once been shining works of craftmanship. The people looked poor and children sat selling strange-looking green things on street corners. These, Tony told her, were 'cactus fruit'. With Tony's help Suzie had managed to successfully get not only her perishable goods, but also a few knick-knacks for the flat. He even carried a large palm plant to the door of the flat for her.

"What's the main office like?" Suzie asked.

"Oh, it's quite posh, I like it," he said. "It's better than the one in the UK. It has been newly done out with marble floors and pillars, air conditioning, cold water on tap, and cookies at break. You'll like it too."

"Sounds marvellous," Suzie said excitedly. "See you on Monday. Thanks for all your help and such a great welcome."

Suzie entered the flat and dumped her shopping. She half expected a 'what time do you call this?' from Isabel but she was still asleep, sprawled out on the bed in the largest bedroom. Isabel must have woken at some point as all of her clothes were neatly folded or set out on hangers, and her suitcase was empty. Her many creams and perfumes were set out with military precision on what passed for a dressing table.

In the lounge area she placed the palm plant this way and that to find the best place for. She put her food items away and had a quick cuppa hoping Isabel would wake soon, but she was still asleep. Forty minutes passed. Suzie jiggled her leg and looked out of all the windows. Curiosity was getting the better of her. Starved of conversation, bristling with excitement, and with nothing better to do Suzie decided to go out again to one of the local shops she had seen on the way back with Tony earlier as it looked like they sold posters. She reasoned that they might have something to brighten the flat up a bit and it might give her an idea of what the local trade was like outside of the souks.

It was an easy five-minute walk and shaded from the sun most of the way by high saffron-coloured walls. Suzie pushed the shop door open, which swung easily. She wandered around the shop browsing. It was not a tourist-type shop in the slightest as there were no English signs up anywhere, so she probably looked a bit out of place. Judging by the posters on the wall (which were all written in French or Arabic) only locals gave it any custom. Suzie had passable French and so managed to work out through a mixture of reading the posters and from what the locals were buying that the greatest trade here was supplying marketing posters to local shopkeepers. Nothing here to brighten up the flat walls – not unless she wanted a poster on 'how to brighten your smile with Ali's toothpaste'. Curiously the shop also sold envelopes and reams and reams of printer paper, which looked a bit out of place.

Suzie hung around at the back of the shop as if deciding upon what to buy so that she could see what the passing trade level was like. In fact, the shop did not seem at all busy but nevertheless there was a queue of people waiting to be served at the till which never seemed to move. She did not speak Arabic but understood perfectly what one of the guys muttered as he walked away from the counter. It was obviously a derogatory comment and no interpretation was needed. She had to agree. The customer service was terrible here, even for locals. The shopkeeper-cum-till worker really needed some customer service advice but remembering her experience in the initial souk she thought better of it and left.

Roll on tomorrow? Roll on Monday! She couldn't wait to start her new job.

Chapter 4

Marrakesh Headquarters

"Come on! Get your butt moving!" Isabel was up bright and early the next morning and had even put some sort of pancakes to warm under the grill. Suzie blinked as the four walls came into focus. Oh yes! She had a brand-new life and swanky new office to work in!

After a refreshing shower, two cups of coffee, and pancakes inside her, she felt ready to take on the world. She didn't think too much about where Isabel found those breakfast items, she was too excited.

Tony was at reception when they arrived at the main office, ready to take them on a tour before showing them where their new line manager sat. The main reception hall was double height, full of marble, with a large marble staircase sweeping up to the first floor. The offices were set in a square around a tiled courtyard. The exterior of the square was built of the local stone, so that from the outside it just looked like a normal Moroccan building. Each office had one wall with a small window high up in the stone wall with expensive-looking art placed below, and two whitewashed walls. The remaining internal wall (and the corridor wall) were completely made of glass so that you could see the internal courtyard from your desk. Seated areas in the courtyard were shaded by gigantic palms, and a fountain tinkled and splattered pleasantly over the walkway. The building was a lovely mixture of modern and traditional Moroccan. All the offices on the second floor had internal balconies facing the courtyard that were wide enough to sit on. Coffee breaks could take on a whole new meaning here! The main office was just as posh as Tony had described it. They finished the welcome tour at the canteen door so it was now time to get down to business. Tony led the way to Eric, their new line manager.

"Welcome to Morocco, ladies. Please take a seat. I've heard a lot about you both. Particularly you, Isabel." Eric gave her a knowing look and she glowed with pride. Eric looked a lot like a bank manager rather than an ad agency boss – smart grey suit, finely groomed appearance with impeccably neat hair, and small silver glasses. He spent the next hour talking about the standards that would be expected, the office ethos, and the importance of filing expenses on time. It was then that he dropped the bombshell. "And of course, Isabel, you will be working here… and you, Suzie, will be working in our other branch." Isabel looked triumphant. The cat had just got the expensive-looking cream and she couldn't be happier. There had been no mention of this back in the UK.

"Other b-branch?" Suzie managed to stutter.

"Yes. It's closer to where your flat is. I will send you

both to that branch tomorrow. The place needs a bit of 'licking into shape' but I am sure you'll be fine." Suzie's heart sank. "But first I want you to do a bit of business tomorrow morning with a shop owner/manager."

Isabel was surprisingly comforting. "I'm sure the other branch is just as nice."

Eric continued, "We have proposed a new ad campaign for the shop owner. Successfully sell it to him, and you will do well here."

At lunch the two friends decided to check out the work canteen/café. This served the most delicious array of cakes that Suzie had ever seen. It had a state-of-the art media suite attached on one side and they realised that they had not been given a full tour of the main branch. They also discovered that it had a spa annex complete with gym, garden, and a pool for employees to use on days off. Suzie fought off thoughts that she had 'lucked out' again. Hopefully her own branch tomorrow would be equally as good but she could see that Isabel was already mentally writing e-mails back to the UK and could guess what would be in them. The cat had not only got the cream but also the salmon mousse and beluga caviar too. Yes, Isabel would be very happy here.

*

Suzie and Isabel were to see Mr Kassab today (a local shop owner and local businessman), in order to help try and grow his business through the ad agency with their latest campaign. Eric, her new line manager, seemed nice enough. He had got them working straight away which

Suzie liked. He had explained that, unlike the UK workday, there was the option here for the workday to be split into two halves (morning and evening with the afternoon free every day). This was to take advantage of working in the cooler part of the day. Suzie could see that this made sense but it had not gone down well with Isabel, so the pair of them had decided to work 9–5pm.

Eric had given them directions on how to get to Mr Kassab's shop and today Suzie arrived first. Isabel had said she just needed to divert on the way to get something from the souk so had told Suzie to carry on without her. To her surprise, Mr Kassab's shop was the same shop she had visited yesterday with the bad customer service. Suzie waited twenty minutes. Where was that girl? Probably haggling some poor guy down on a price somewhere or checking out the best shopping bargains. Despite the relatively short walk from HQ, her feet seemed tired today so she sat on the small flat stone wall facing the shop. It was just under hip height and warm to the touch from the sunshine. She quickly realised that the wall provided a great viewing point not only of the shop, but also down the street in two different directions. The foliage from the palm above gave some welcome shade so it was the perfect place to wait and watch.

Outside the shop was a constant flow of people: those checking prices on shop windows, a man who seemed to be asking for directions, a woman who was loaded down with honey, and a few customers who obviously knew the man in the shop very well as they seemed to be just talking with him. Amongst the constant flurry of feet and shop customers (who came out with posters), there were what appeared to be shop 'runners'. In England they would be called 'gofers' (cheap labour running errands).

Suzie tossed her hair back and repositioned her sunglasses as a welcome breeze momentarily brushed her face. This was the life! She was getting paid to wait here in the sunshine. This was the nicest thing that had happened to Suzie all week, discounting the cakes in HQ's canteen that is. She imagined how a crisp white Chardonnay or cold lemonade would feel right now. In her mind's eye she could see the beads of condensation forming on the glass from the chilled drink. She could even hear the clink of ice cubes and imagined raising the glass to her lips. A slice of lemon bobbed gently up and down. Back in reality, a small delicate caterpillar was inching its way quietly along the wall.

"Daydreaming again I see." It was Isabel. "You'll never get anywhere like that. You have to be sharp and focused at all times to get anywhere in this world. I've told you that before." She flung her bag down on the wall and stood looking at the shop for a split second. Turning back to the wall and Suzie, Isabel had a look of disgust on her face. With one blow she crushed the caterpillar dead. "Come on, we can't wait here all day."

Irritated by Isabel's impatience and inhumanity, Suzie followed her into the shop. The man behind the counter beamed at Isabel, greeted her warmly, and then asked them to follow him through to the back. Suzie had to resist the urge to suddenly shout 'mass butterfly murderer!', so instead she smoothed down the material of her pencil skirt before she sat down. The man introduced himself as Mr Kassab and started to make pleasantries but Isabel cut across him almost immediately.

"So you want to keep all of your old customers and make room for new ones under the new proposed campaign – is that right?" Before he could respond she was talking again. "Well that isn't how it generally works I'm afraid. We have research that shows us that with the new ad campaign you will get a better brand of customer. But obviously it's your choice." Isabel beamed at him, believing that she had instantly won him over. Suzie looked at him. The 'shutters' had come down in his eyes. She knew immediately that they would never see his account in their in-tray again despite his forced smile. Isabel bounced out of the shop leaving a wave of Calvin Klein's latest perfume in her wake. Suzie felt sorry for the shopkeeper, said goodbye, and headed back to the flat to get something to eat. Suzie was confused. She had thought they were going to see her branch today, but Eric had given them the rest of the day off after this business interaction to get to know the local customs. Perhaps she had misheard? To Isabel, 'getting to know the local customs' meant 'you've got free time to do what you want' but to Suzie that meant 'find out how people live here'. She noticed that Isabel had started disappearing for small amounts of time without explanation, just like she did in the UK. Goodness knows what she was doing. Maybe shopping, but Suzie decided it was probably best not to ask.

*

Back at the agency HQ office the next day Suzie was hoping it was her turn to see her new luxury branch. Life was looking up at last! Mum would not believe it.

On the walk up to Eric's office, Suzie spotted a photo of the second ad agency branch on the lobby wall. She was relieved to see that it looked fairly posh, not as big as the headquarters here, but things were looking hopeful all the same.

As they entered the office, Eric smiled the kind of smarmy smile at them that made Suzie want to mimic being sick into the wastepaper bin, but she restrained herself.

"Morning, ladies."

"Morning," they chorused back.

"How did the meeting with Mr Kassab go yesterday?"

"It was a breeze," Isabel stated. "I think he has seen sense, and his ideas will now be more in line with our main focus." Suzie kept silent.

"Marvelous, just what I like to hear." Eric seemed delighted. "That's just as well because that is where you will be working, Suzie."

"What?" Suzie exclaimed. "I thought that was just a bit of business yesterday? The shop looks nothing like the picture in the lobby of the other branch. They are not even remotely similar."

"Oh that? That was taken years ago. It has had a face lift, several repaints, and an extension knocked down since that was taken. Not to mention two past owners." The word 'damn' didn't seem strong enough now. Double damn! The second branch was really only a failing shop with bad customer service. Not only was this where she was going to have to work but Isabel had just screwed it all up for her, going in like a bull in a china shop, alienating the shop owner and probably the staff too. Trust Isabel to get the better deal. There would be no veranda coffee breaks, pleasant courtyards, or delicious cakes for Suzie. Suzie's bright future was dimming by the second. Eric continued, "I also want you to go and tell Mr Kassab that following our successful takeover bid he will no longer be the manager there. He's good with the locals but neglects the bigger business. He won't be pleased as he was hoping to remain 'top dog', but he will get over it."

"Me? What me? Me... tell him?" Suzie was dumbstruck.

"Yes, you. Think you can handle that?"

"I... er..."

"Just say if you can't..." He was watching her face now. How dare he put her in this position during her first few days here! Isabel just sat there silent. Suzie looked back at Eric.

After a moment's thought, Suzie said, "It's just that I think it would be better coming from you as you already know Mr Kassab."

"Oh." Eric was now clearly annoyed, and Suzie could see that she had just failed her first test. Triple damn. "Well now that you have seen where each other will be working you will appreciate that your two roles will be slightly different. Suzie, you will serve your two-week induction period here after which you will move to the other branch. You will, of course, continue to have good links here and report back to me. Occasionally you will be required to work here when we have the big campaigns going on as it is 'all hands to the pump' at those times. All clear?" Suzie nodded. Quadruple damn. What was she going to do now?

Chapter 5

Settling In

The two induction weeks at headquarters passed all too quickly and Suzie felt sad leaving Isabel, the swanky surroundings, and after-work spa treatments behind, not to mention the canteen cakes which tasted even better than they looked. The two friends didn't know many people here yet but that did not stop Isabel throwing a couple of lively staff parties back at the flat.

Despite her best efforts, Suzie's talks with Mr Kassab at the shop did not go well. She couldn't blame him. It seemed she was to run his shop in his place. He had, to all intents and purposes, been thrown out of his managerial role by her without notice. Thrown out by a foreign woman who had tried to convince him it was not her fault, and that he should stay on and work for her. He told her that women did not do that sort of thing around here and she should be ashamed. Even though it was not her doing she had to admit he had a point. Trusted business partners, whatever their gender, just did not do that to each other.

Suzie felt that Eric, her new line manager, had pushed her out onto a very precarious 'limb' and was ready to retreat from her at a moment's notice if things turned nasty. Because of this she knew instinctively that no real support would ever be forthcoming from him. Suzie breathed a sigh of relief when Mr Kassab just walked out of the shop without even looking back and did not return. She would have done the same if roles had been reversed.

Suzie quickly realised that the remaining shop staff were not going to like a woman being in charge either. They were unaccustomed to 'taking orders' or even suggestions from a woman, let alone a foreign one. But still, she was now their boss. She explained that she was there to help and had no wish to upset anyone, but this talk did not go any better. One guy was muttering in the corner in Arabic when she gathered them together. On interrogating one of the others later they translated this as 'too late, English slime'. She didn't blame him either.

With impeccable timing Isabel had then texted her to say how wonderfully her day was going. To make matters worse, Eric had just e-mailed her to say that she would need to 'sell contracts' here in the shop. There had been no mention of that during induction. Back in the UK they had a separate team doing that. For all she knew there *was* a team at HQ and Isabel would be making full use of them no doubt. When Suzie queried this Eric confirmed that this was the case, but due to the fact that the shop used to have Mr Kassab doing that (and he was now gone) Suzie should do it herself. What the hell had she got herself into? What had they been thinking in the UK to send her here? Was she being sent down with the sinking ship? Surely there were people back in the UK that would have been better suited to all this?

*

Later that day, the two friends compared notes back at the flat. Isabel went to great lengths complaining about the shade of her welcome banner on her desk and how it clashed with the colour of her scarf. She was also complaining about how Suzie was the boss and she, Isabel, just had two admin people at the Moroccan headquarter branch. No-one had set out a welcome banner on Suzie's desk, quite the reverse. After twenty minutes of listening to Isabel droning on about how unfair it all was, Suzie made an excuse to go ring her boyfriend.

"Have you set the world on fire yet?" he snarled. His tone was cold.

"No... not yet..." She told him about her first couple of weeks and neither of them mentioned that he had not bothered to come to the airport with her, or to say goodbye.

He sighed. "Well... I guess you will be back soon, won't you?" There was no 'How are you?' or 'What's it like?'. A 'Sorry, love you' would have been nice but there was nothing.

Suzie hesitated. "No, I won't be returning just yet. I will let you know when there are any fixed dates."

"Oh."

She mentioned about having to sell contracts here but before she could comment he said, "What you? You? Sell contracts?"

She made an excuse and ended the call. It was going to take him a while to get used to this newfound long-distance relationship of theirs. Her mother was expecting a call from her tonight but at this point she could not face another 'I told you so' voice at the other end of the phone so decided to put it off until tomorrow.

After a perfunctory meal of bread and fruit, Suzie set about forming ideas about how to take the scruffy shop forward and turn it into a proper ad agency. A proper 'going concern'. She supposed she had better make the best of it while it lasted. Isabel was now reading over her shoulder.

"Rather you than me," she said.

"Yeah thanks." Suzie screwed up her face and threw a crumpled ball of paper at her.

"I think I'd better help you with that before a mountain of rejected ideas completely smothers you!" Isabel laughed.

"Ha, ha, funny girl." Suzie started jotting down some more ideas to improve sales and Isabel chipped in with ideas here and there. By the end of the evening Suzie had a makeshift sales and contracts strategy. Only one problem though: it depended upon having a large bank of photos to use at a moment's notice. There was no-one at the shop that could currently do that (except a seventy-year-old incumbent who would not be at all eager to take that on). However, this strategy was the only one she had. One problem at a time! She would now be able to go back to the 'delectable Eric' with her plan. They both celebrated by cracking open the last bottle of Prosecco that they had bought with them from the UK.

At 6am the next morning a distant sound of singing had awoken Suzie at sunrise and she was intrigued. She got up and tried to locate where the singing was coming from by looking out of the living room window, but the angle was wrong. This must be the daily call to prayer Tony had told her about. She had not noticed it up to now as they had both slept until 7am each day.

A little later, while she was still sitting by the lounge window, she noticed a small swarthy man of around sixty appeared to the right down below in the small, cobbled alley to the side of the flat. He was dressed in local attire with a white turban. He had a cart loaded up with rugs and carpets which he slowly pushed up the slight incline. He walked as if he had all the time in the world. She watched as he laid out his wares in the street down below their first-floor flat. Everyone else on the streets appeared to be heading for the souks.

*

The next few days passed slowly for Suzie at the shop, and each were filled was discontented grunts and staff disappearing off for tea breaks without telling her. She was doing her best to put the new sales plan into action but the staff were not making it easy for her.

She had started to have breakfast each day on the flat balcony before work and she noticed that the 'carpet man' (as she was now calling him) came most days at 7am to set up his carpet and rug stall in the side street below their flat. She noticed at weekends he always took the stall down at midday and disappeared back down the slight incline with his cart. In the days that followed, this 'watching-the-carpet-man' ritual gave her sense of security that some things in the world do not change. His appearance was like clockwork, which meant that by the time he was opposite her flat it was time to get ready for work.

On some days other stalls would randomly pop out of nowhere and disappear just as quickly. Today was just such a day. A second stall had been set up just a little further away so Suzie decided she would leave the house a little early today to see what the new stall was selling. As usual, the carpet man was down there too.

"Wow." The new stall was selling what looked like polished fossils. She picked up a small palm-sized, beige, stone-coloured object with a high-gloss sheen. It was an ammonite. Suzie had never seen anything like it. She paid for it without the customary local haggling and stood looking at its many segments shining in the sun. The carpet man, on the next stall along, interrupted her thoughts.

"Miss. Can I look?" Suzie handed him the ammonite. He turned it over and over in his hands as if examining it with X-ray eyes. "You know it has become this smooth by being beaten by the wind and sand for many years, don't you?" he said. Suzie looked at it more intently. "See that little groove there?" he pointed out a small chink in the structure with his little finger. "That's not damage from someone…" He mimicked someone dropping it with a look of surprise on their face. "That's where the animal had some sort of injury when it was alive. It's shell was broken there. But of course..." he spread his arms open wide "...that was many millions of years ago. Intriguing, no?"

"Definitely!" Suzie said. She found him intriguing too. His swarthy brown skin had collected a few wrinkles over time. He had unfathomable brown eyes which looked at you with a gaze that was deep and mysterious. Somehow the meaning behind the eyes did not feel hidden or secret, but instead, they engendered trust. She wondered if he had been selling carpets all his life but thought it would be rude to ask. Instead, she thanked him and continued walking down the narrow-cobbled alley that led to the shop.

*

In the days that followed the carpet man seemed to be popping up everywhere: the city gate, his customary place in the street by her flat, and even the shop. He came in wanting some photocopies for his business.

Carpet Man called her to one side. "You know people have been saying that bad things will happen with a woman in charge don't you? Mr Kassab was liked around here. A very respectable man."

She stumbled a little. This shocked her. "I-I am truly sorry on behalf of the agency. I didn't know you knew him. I was aware he was no longer the manager, but the decision was not my doing. I had no idea they were going to do something like that to such a nice family man." Carpet Man looked quizzically at Suzie's face. For a reason that Suzie did not yet fully understand, she let her guard down. "I know that I am a 'fish out of water'. No wonder the locals hate me." Again, he was studying her face.

"Don't worry, I myself have been a 'fish out of water', as you say. Give them time, I am sure they will like you better when they see how brilliant you are at business." He had a twinkle in his eye now. Despite his bad news she felt a slight bond forming. She wanted to trust him.

"You will have to teach me about business first!" She laughed.

*

The shop staff continued to go in and out of the shop all day without Suzie's consent despite constant and explicit instructions not to do so. She had never been a line manager before and knew she was woefully inadequate. The newly promoted shop deputy manager was at least seventy and had been missing for two hours. When he came back he was his usual unpleasant self. She noticed that he followed this up with several long and secretive talks on the phone, but the shop staff refused to tell her who he was talking to or what was going on. Suzie decided it must be local contacts which the staff were not yet trusting her with but for all she knew it could be personal calls. The fact that she could speak a little French did not seem to help alleviate the situation either. Towards the end of the afternoon the staff rounded on Suzie with what was obviously a planned manoeuvre. They asked her straight out if she was any good at her job.

"Of course I am!" she said. "Do you think they would put a woman in charge if I was not worth two men?" She sounded way more confident than she felt. Stray wisps of her curly hair kept escaping from her hair clip and dangling annoyingly in front of her face as she spoke. Her reassurance had not had the desired effect as the staff became ruder and more hostile over the remainder of the working day. Language was definitely a problem.

"Can I help you?" Suzie barked at the next customer without looking up. It turned out not to be a 'next customer' at all, but a friendly looking guy in his thirties. He had short brown hair, a tanned face, and wore a dark shirt and shorts. A blue camera bag was slung over his shoulder and he had an impressive array of camera gear around his neck. He looked Moroccan but introduced himself as Andy. When he saw the slightly puzzled look on Suzie's face he explained that his mother was English and his father Moroccan, and that he did the odd bit of photography for the owner here. He therefore wondered whether she, who was obviously now the new manager, would like to see some of his work. As the current shop photographer (and newly promoted deputy manager) was the wrong side of seventy and stubbornly belligerent, she could see why Andy's services had been needed here from time to time. Andy offered to do some 'live action' photography with Suzie right then and there at the souk. As the workday was almost at an end and the shop's deputy manager usually did the locking up, she took him up on his offer.

As they walked he shot pictures and every now and then he showed her what he had taken on the camera's flip-out viewscreen. He was good! There was pleasant banter about the setting up of shots, and fifty minutes later they were back outside the shop. Andy promised to return the next day with all the photos on a USB stick.

*

Early the next morning Andy arrived as promised and picked up two posters from the shop's deputy manager that he had ordered yesterday. He then gave Suzie a USB stick and a folder of 'stills' to look at.

"Not bad," she muttered. He had caught the locals in candid shots all over the souk and the depth of field was amazing. A shot of an angry man behind a stall berating a customer caught Suzie's eye. It was the same guy that had been rude to her the first day she was here! Andy noticed the look on Suzie's face. "Oh, that's Titch," he said. "Or at least that's what I call him. Everyone knows Titch."

"Why 'Titch'? He's not that small. He's quite tall."

Andy laughed a full belly laugh but did not explain. "I know him well. Probably best to avoid him if I were you. He can be quite nasty."

"Yep, already sussed that one," she said.

"Good for you." He handed Suzie two tubes of cardboard with the posters inside.

"What's this?"

"For you."

"Me?"

"Yes, why don't you open them?" Suzie was curious so popped open the end part and slid the contents out onto the serving desk. She unrolled two identical-looking rolls of paper and she could see they were actually candid shots of herself. He had captured her with really expressive looks on her face, one laughing with the locals, and one perplexed at Moroccan pricing. He had actually made her look presentable. "You can put them up on your wall if you like?" he continued. "The locals like shots like that."

"I... er... thank you," said Suzie. She was genuinely touched. "Oh... by the way... my name is Suzie, Suzie Watson... in case no-one has told you that yet." The agency had certainly not told *her* very much about who did what around here.

"Andy, Andy Ahmed. Pleased to make your acquaintance." He did a mock bow.

Eric had made it clear that she was to make whatever decisions were necessary. She must be doing something right as takings had been up a little over the last two weeks, so she asked Andy to come back and do some casual work in a couple of weeks' time. He was thrilled.

Chapter 6

Shopping at the Souk

"Oh, come on Isabel, it will be fun…" Suzie tried to coax her out of the chair to come round the souks with her but Isabel remained resolute with her feet curled under her, like a cat. This was her customary pose at this time of day. Isabel said she wanted to get her nails done at HQ's spa later so Suzie left the flat in mock indignation. "When I come back with a Prada handbag at a rock-bottom price, don't say I didn't warn you!" So much for girlie shopping trips and 'girl power'!

As always, the souk was a feast for the senses. Today it was colourful pashminas, chickens running loose in the meat section, and a snake charmer whose snake was having a break (or at least that's what the owner said). Suzie had spotted a handbag stall the day before and made a beeline for that, but it was situated on the far side of the souk that Tony had shown her. She wanted to send some snazzy-looking bags back to England for her mum and sister. After ten minutes browsing other stalls on the way, she realised that a young lad seemed to be following her and entreating her for something. She could not speak his language and tried to ignore him but he became very insistent. As his desperation got greater his variety of language got greater too, but Suzie could understand nothing of what he was saying. She assumed that he was pursuing her to make a sale as she had heard about tactics like this at the office. She quickened her pace and suddenly felt very vulnerable as a lone female. A further few steps later he hit upon English, looked at her with large brown eyes, and said simply, "Please help."

Guarded, she stopped and turned around. "What's the problem?"

"Come," he said excitedly and beckoned Suzie over to his stall. Thinking that this was still probably an oblique way of getting a sale that she was not about to give him, she figured there would be no harm so she followed him. "I make you mint tea," he stated. Intrigued, she trailed along behind him into the back part of the stall where he had a small stove set up. She had never seen anything like this. Suzie had her back to the exit and made sure he never got between her and the exit. She wasn't stupid. "*Parlez vous Français?*" he enquired.

"I speak a little French," Suzie replied. He was delighted. He explained in French that English was his fifth language so he wasn't too good. French was his second language so it was much easier for him to explain what he needed in French. Suzie marvelled at his language prowess and went along with it. As they talked it became obvious that he was genuinely in a fix and Suzie relaxed and sat down. It transpired that he had fallen in love with an English girl who had been here on holiday that year. They had been writing to each other ever since, and he lived for her return. However, her grandfather had become sick and he wanted to send her some herbs to help her grandfather recover. The boy smiled and said that that was where she came in. As his written English was bad, he said he wanted to dictate a letter in French so that Suzie could write it in English. He handed her a paper and pen and they got to work. The letter was a heartfelt piece of prose. He longed to see his girlfriend. This was teenage love at its best. She realised that she had been wrong to misjudge him as he had made no move to sell her anything, but instead thanked her copiously by weighing her down with gifts from his stall: four bags of delicious mint tea (mint, and three herbs she didn't recognise); a natural shampoo-type herb; and a bag of multicoloured spices. Slightly stunned by his generosity, she thanked him and made her way out to the front of the stall.

"*À bientôt! Merci!*" He shouted after her.

Suzie made her way back to the flat through the bustling crowd, forgetting completely about her handbag quest. How strange. The boy's stall had no soundproofing as it was only made of canvas, but she had been oblivious to the noise on the street the whole time whilst inside. Time seemed to stand still. The boy was still waving furiously from his stall, and she had obviously made his day.

Isabel was not there when Suzie got back.

*

Later that day, Suzie told Isabel about her little adventure but she was not amused. "You stupid little idiot! Quite apart from the danger you put yourself in, he is probably a drug runner sending 'wacky baccy' to his pushers in the UK. You are implicated now because you wrote the letter. You had better watch your back." That stung, but Isabel was probably right. How could she have been so stupid? Maybe she should go with Tony to the souk next time.

*

The very next day Suzie decided to get back on the horse and had asked for Tony's help. He was always so accommodating and said yes immediately. Suzie thought about the early morning fruit-and-veg markets back home which was the closest thing she had seen to the souks here. Crates would bang and crash, and a melee of indistinct yells would travel far in the cold morning air. Disgruntled instructions to pallet loaders would be heard, and the sound of wood against metal and metal against cobbled stones. The echoing of voices, indistinct thuds, occasional jeers from fellow workers, and the sounds of hydraulics loading the vans would disrupt the peace. Back home, the darkness, tradespeople, and general public shopping in bulk at some unearthly hour all seemed to add to the feeling of clandestine shopping there. Here in Morocco, it could not have been more different. It was sunny, warm, and open. The vibrant colours made you feel alive. They positively smacked you in the face.

"Oh, look at that!" Suzie pointed to a beautifully coloured rug draped in the window of a shop.

Tony bent over to look. "Too late, he's seen you." The shopkeeper came rushing out to make his sale.

"Come," he said, "you buy…" and tried to usher them into the shop. Suzie was becoming a little more proficient at ducking and diving shopkeepers wanting a sale, but the shopkeeper grabbed her right arm and would not let go. To her horror she could not escape.

"Ah…" he was now stroking her long curly blonde hair and she felt slightly sick as he did so.

The shopkeeper looked at Tony and said, "I give you five camels for this one?"

Tony had a look of suppressed mischief on his face. "Well…" he said, tilting his head to one side. He pretended he was thinking about it.

"Don't you dare sell me for five camels, Tony!" Suzie exclaimed. "I happen to know that the going rate is seven. Don't you dare!"

"Erm…" Tony stroked his chin with one hand, but Suzie noticed that he kept his other hand firmly on her left forearm. The shopkeeper tugged on Suzie's arm a little harder and Tony pulled back on her left. She was beginning to feel like a piece of meat in a tug-of-war game.

"Tony…" she warned, eyebrows knitting in panic now.

"No," Tony announced. "I will keep her. Five camels are not enough."

The shopkeeper let go with a sigh.

When they were safely out of earshot Suzie swotted Tony over the back of his head. "Five camels indeed!"

"Whaaaaaat?" Tony exclaimed in mock surprise. "You know I wouldn't have sold you for less than six, don't you?" Suzie swotted him over the head again. "Gerrrroff, you 'six-camel' swotting-type woman!"

Chapter 7

Business the Moroccan Way

Carpet Man had asked to meet with her today, but Suzie wondered if he would actually arrive as his cart had been missing from outside the flat over the last few days. The time for her lunch break came and she went out to meet him at the agreed point outside her shop. He was there. "Hi, been anywhere nice?" she enquired.

"Where? That is not important." His liquid brown eyes were not guarded, despite his enigmatic response. "You travel. Yes." This was not a question but a statement. "You travel... and so do I." He explained about the nomadic nature of Berbers and the Imazighen lifestyle.

She didn't quite know why he had asked to meet her or why he had told her to sit on the grey wall facing the shop and watch what people were doing across the square. But intrigued, she did as she was asked.

All she could see was an old woman struggling with three rolled-up posters. Each time she wrestled them under control, one end of a tube would swing out and she would drop at least two of the rolls. The paper was becoming crumpled already and the woman had not even got them home yet. Carpet Man followed her eyes.

She then saw a man coming out of her own shop door with his hands full of copier paper. The paper bag he was carrying tore as the half open door fell back on him before he was fully through. He too dropped some of his wares as they slid through the open crack in the paper bag. She was embarrassed. "Can't someone hold the door open for him and give him a proper bag to take home?"

"Ah, now you *see*. Business is not just about selling your product. It is about courtesy and packaging too." Suzie realised that this was in fact a business lesson. She had been joking when she had said 'teach me business' but he was serious and had taken up the challenge. She made a mental note to buy some cardboard tubes and biodegradable plastic bags immediately. "What else do you see?" he said.

Suzie scanned the marketplace. For one heart-stopping moment she thought she saw her boyfriend amongst the busy throng of people. Her mind must be playing some kind of Freudian trick on her. She was beginning to enjoy herself and had only once thought about her boyfriend since she got here. Perhaps this was her innermost self, surfacing to remind her that she had unresolved business back home? After all, it was round about now that she had told her boyfriend that she would be returning to the UK and had not given him a firm return date yet. "Get a grip," she scolded herself. She noticed that some stalls were more popular with Western-looking tourists, others with the locals so she said so. Carpet Man was encouraging.

"Good. Good. What else?"

A group of young European lads were haggling at one stall. When they had bought the item they wanted they walked away boasting about their haggling prowess. However, the stallholder hung his head. Suzie continued, "I see that most Europeans do not haggle like the locals and when they try it, they go too far. They insult the poor stallholder."

"Excellent! You have learnt business lesson number one – Courtesy, packaging, and honour. We will do lesson number two next week."

*

"Yoohoo!" Isabel called as she entered the flat. "Anyone home?"

"In here," Suzie replied.

Isabel appeared laden with heavy bags and looked excited. "Come on Suzie, help me decorate the flat. I've asked a few people from HQ over for a party. I found a great shop where you can buy all sorts of party stuff. It was hard to find but look at this!" She held out a small, delicately made camel covered with minute paper loops in rainbow colours.

"What are they?" Suzie asked.

"Placeholders. Aren't they great? And look at these…" She held out intricately patterned tiles for Suzie to inspect. "Coasters. I love that shop!"

They put on some tracks from Isabel's Spotify and got to work hanging up paper lanterns and decorating the table. They laid out trays of beautifully decorated canapes that Isabel had bought, which Suzie had to admit, looked fab. Isabel had a real eye for that sort of thing.

Just after Isabel had changed, there was a knock at the door. "Come on in!" Isabel shouted. "Grab yourself a drink. There's wine in the cooler or cocktails if you want." Five people from HQ streamed in the door, some of which Suzie had seen before.

"Where did you get all this alcohol, Isabel?" Suzie asked.

"Ask me no questions and I will tell you no lies!" Isabel picked up a cocktail, completed it with mini umbrella, and started dancing to the music. She looked great in her royal-blue satin crop top and trousers. Suzie had not changed or done her make-up yet, so she still had her lightweight jogging pants on. After a quick change into a party outfit, Suzie joined the ten-strong throng that was now pulsating with the music.

*

For Suzie's second business lesson the next day the carpet man invited her to sit in on one of his business meetings. She groaned silently as she nursed her aching head and gathered from the little 'French' she knew that he was telling his business associates he was 'trying out the European idea of having a secretary'. He motioned to Suzie. She grinned inwardly but lowered her eyes as he had shown her to do and nodded her head to them. They looked uncertainly at him as business was usually a male affair, but begrudgingly allowed her in. The whole thing took place in semi darkness with heavy curtains pulled across the windows to keep the heat and dust out. Carpet Man spent most of his time during the meeting smoking a Turkish pipe with the men, nodding here and there. He seemed to know instinctively what needed to be done. The meeting ended and Carpet Man and Suzie went back to her shop.

"What did you think?" he said simply.

"Not sure. It was not like any board meeting I have ever been to!"

He laughed. "No – not like board meetings. I said very little. Did you notice?"

"Yes. The other guy did most of the talking. I wasn't expecting that."

"Little was said but much was accomplished. So... what is lesson number two?"

"Er... I guess it is really important to listen to your business associates..."

"Yes... that is a large part of it. I do not usually smoke but did so because he was expecting it. Do you understand that?"

"Yes. You made him relax."

"I was determined to get a certain result and did not give up... I let him talk, feel relaxed..."

"You made him feel comfortable and he ended up agreeing with you..."

"Yes – that is excellent, Berber Girl, truly excellent."

"Thank you, Carpet Man." Suzie gulped and covered her mouth. She was instantly aware that she had actually said 'Carpet Man' out loud.

"What is that you call me?" He laughed. She was too embarrassed to speak. "Okay," he said. "I will be your carpet man. Carpet Man and Berber Girl make a good business team, no?"

Ten minutes after the carpet man had left the shop, Suzie found a letter addressed to her. It was from Jai, an Indian guy that had worked at the shop for two years, who Suzie had put in charge of sales. His letter was short and simple. It described how his father back in India was dying, and how he had now left his job to do his 'sonly' duties. After the initial settling-in period when things seemed to be going a little better with the shop employees, many had inexplicably left to find other jobs. Jai was the last remaining permanent staff. This now only left Suzie with a seventy-year-old photographer-cum-deputy manager, and just a few casual staff to run the whole thing.

Within minutes the phone rang and it was Eric her line manager. Perfect timing as ever. "So... now that Jai has left, what are you going to do about it?" How did he know so quickly? She would have to be careful – he was always so quick to criticise.

"I'm not sure... I... er..."

"Well, you'd better sort it out sharpish... You've had a whole month to think about it during his notice period. We *do* have a business to run you know."

So... Jai had told *Eric* he was leaving but hadn't mentioned it to Suzie. Typical. And with no sales manager now she would have to do it. Great. She thought she had been getting somewhere, with Jai, at least. She didn't mention to Eric that she did not know Jai was leaving because he would think her pathetic, with no control over her own employees. Settling for 'unorganised' in his eyes was much better.

Over a cool glass of prosecco that evening, Suzie told Isabel about her troublesome staff. Inwardly she knew she needed to show some of that quiet determination that Carpet Man had shown during his business meeting. She jumped up, stuck a Post-it on the fridge saying: 'Passivity is banned!', and poured herself another glass of wine to drown her sorrows.

*

Next morning, there was a young girl selling some kind of fruit outside the flat. Suzie had seen her several times before. She was a small, thin, but pretty-looking girl of around twelve years old and today she was wearing a scruffy blue dress and headscarf. Her dusty feet and ankles were bare. She had set up a stall next to the carpet man, however the word 'stall' was a bit of an overstatement. It consisted of a small and battered wooden folding table, and a tray loaded with oval 'green things'. Suzie was intrigued. She said goodbye to Isabel who was singing in the shower and banged the flat door shut. Downstairs she wandered over to the girl, but she shrunk back a little when Suzie approached her.

"What are these?" she asked Carpet Man, pointing at the strange-looking objects on the girl's tray.

"Cactus fruit," he explained.

"What do they taste like?"

"Many people love them." Suzie must have looked doubtful so he paid the girl some dirham, flicked open a knife from his pocket, slit the fruit open, and offered half to Suzie. "Here… eat the fleshy part."

It was amazingly juicy. The flavour was a bit of an acquired taste, but she could see how refreshing these would be in the desert.

"Thank you," she said.

The girl seemed to be asking the carpet man if she could go somewhere, and he nodded. She skipped off happily without a care in the world.

"Is that your daughter?" Suzie asked.

"No – not my daughter! She is a – how you say – orphan. I am teaching her how to run a business to make a living. She makes a little every day and will earn more now that she has this spot. You could learn from her, no?" Suzie's hackles rose slightly because he had suggested that she could learn from a twelve-year-old child, but listened all the same as he described how the girl had come to be in Marrakesh after both of her parents had disappeared. It was a heart-wrenching story.

Suzie decided to tell him about the business problems she was having, and for the first time his words made her stop in her tracks.

"You are fortunate to have a job like you do! Most women do not have jobs like that here – only men. You should enjoy it." He motioned to the little cactus girl. "This girl has nothing but is happy enough."

He was right.

*

With no Jai there to serve the regulars, the morning's work at the shop was busy so it passed quickly enough. As the afternoon break was nearing Suzie realised she hadn't once thought about her initial disappointment at being sent here to the shop instead of the swanky main office. In fact, she had hardly thought about the UK at all since she got here. Andy the photographer turned out to be very dependable. He pitched in to fill most of the small outstanding jobs, and today he had even made a passable lunch for them both.

A young man entered the shop. "Sorry we are closed for lunch," Suzie said.

"Yes – I know," he replied. "Isabel has sent me over to work with you." Suzie took the papers he held in his outstretched hand and realised that he was one of the two admin assistants that worked with Isabel at the main office. She guessed that Isabel heard about Jai leaving and had sent over her 'cast-offs'? Cheek!

"I will have to interview you," Suzie said.

"Okay."

"Follow me." His manner during the interview was unconfident and not at all the kind of person that Isabel would like. Suzie could see immediately why he would not live up to Isabel's expectations. However, he seemed a genuine kind of guy and his work history was good, so she took him on.

Over the next few days that passed Ahmed was shaping up nicely. She used the business lessons Carpet Man had given her to train him in sales, and he learned quickly. Even the locals seemed to like him. Carpet Man's wrinkled brown face appeared at the window, smiling. Suzie waved him in.

"I have something for you," he said, smiling. "I think you will like it." He unrolled a large piece of paper on the counter filled with scribbles and diagrams. Suzie asked Ahmed to make some mint tea and announced that she was not to be disturbed as she was about to have a business meeting with a valued client. She opened out the roll of paper on the table nearby and Carpet Man sat down.

"But this is a whole sales plan for the shop…"

"You like it?" he said apprehensively.

"I do… but…"

"Ah… you don't like it."

"I do… but it is so *strategic*. Sorry… I don't mean to insult you. I am just surprised, that's all. You seem to do your business so intuitively. I didn't think that you thought this way."

"Good business needs both, no?"

"Yes… I'm sure your right… as usual!" She smiled. "I will have a really good look at this. Thank you."

"A gift for my Berber girl… from her Carpet Man." He cocked his head to one side. "I may expect payment for this…" He was joking now.

"I will give you all the royalties you could ever dream of…" Suzie laughed. "But payment will come in the form of copier paper…"

"No problem…" he said. "I like copier paper… it has lots of uses…"

Chapter 8

A Week Full of Surprises

Since putting Carpet Man's sales plan into action, sales were picking up steadily. Suzie had even been able to put together a mini ad campaign with Ahmed's help. Now that the shop had a working sales programme and relatively happy staff, things were starting to take shape at last. Even Eric had allowed Suzie to present her shop figures to the regional managers in HQ's boardroom that week. Suzie couldn't have been happier. Then, to top it all, Christine surprised Suzie with a flying visit one weekend.

"Do you wanna see my shop?" Suzie asked. Christine nodded. "Come on then, it's not far."

Christine stared at the view once inside. "Wowsers, Suzie! What a great job you are doing."

"Really? It's been a very hard slog."

"Well, it's been worth it – the shop looks inviting now. Not like the original photos you sent me. Who did these photos on the wall?"

"Andy." Suzie told Christine about how the sales plan

was starting to take off with more advertising contracts now.

"Did Jai leave you a sales plan?"

"No, I did it…"

"What? Suzie who can't sell heaters to frozen Innuits…?"

"The very same!"

"Wowsers, girl. Total wowsers! Go girl!"

"I admit I had a lot of help, a *lot* of help from certain quarters."

"Even so… tote amazeballs. Proper little entrepreneur, aren't you? So, what's Isabel got to say to about that then?"

"Dunno really. She was a bit miffed at first but seems to be happy enough now. Actually, I haven't seen her this week because she moved out of the flat last weekend. Said something about 'not being able to stand the shabby state of the flat any longer'…"

"Bit sudden wasn't it? Ah well… she always was a snob that girl. All the better for the raucous evening I have planned for you! Come here!" They returned to the flat linked arm in arm and Suzie prepared a quick meal which they ate on the flat's balcony. Neither remembered what happened next but a silly drinking game must have followed as they both nursed a massive hangover the next morning. Before they knew it, Christine was back on the plane flying home, and it had gone all too quickly.

*

The next day after work Suzie supposed she should pick up her mobile to call her mother. She had been putting it off for weeks. "Hi, Mum."

"Oh, hello, dear... remembered you had a mother, I suppose?" Suzie ignored the initial hostility and told her about the massive headway she had made with the shop. "Yes, that's nice, dear. Isabel said she had sent you some help..." That was just like Mum. Giving all credit to Isabel even though she had very little to do with it. What was Isabel doing talking to her mum anyway?

"Thought you may want to know your daughter's doing great things here..." Suzie continued.

"Yes, yes. Isabel says you don't have everything in place like she does but... you are getting by."

It was no used continuing the conversation. "Bye, Mum."

"Bye, dear... and do talk to that poor boyfriend of yours. He's really pining for you..."

"He wasn't when I left..."

"But I am sure he must miss you, dear..."

"Whatever." Suzie touched the keypad and rang off. *Is dialling your mother this hard for everyone?* she wondered.

The flat seemed quiet without Isabel, not that she made loads of noise. Suzie missed the excited chatter about the souks and Isabel's wild plans to take over the company. "You'll see," Isabel had said. "I will be the first woman CEO within three years." Suzie picked up the discarded stockings Isabel had left strewn on the living room floor, washed Isabel's dirty cups (as she obviously wasn't coming back for them now), and went outside to tidy the balcony. Her eye fell upon the cactus girl outside. She was back!

Suzie ran down to the front door and over to the girl. This time the girl did not flee but instead seemed to be looking for the carpet man. *"Je suis désolé, je ne sais pas où l'homme des tapis est. Il n'est pas ici."* The girl looked as if she was going to cry and began to tell Suzie in French that she needed to work to feed her family. Without the carpet man, any other traders would chase her away.

"Your family?" Suzie asked, alarmed. "How old are you?"

"Twelve," the girl said. "My sister is eight and I have to look after her. We have no-one else." Suzie stroked her hair in sympathy. Could this really be true? The girl continued, "If you like, I could follow your tall friend and tell you where she goes?"

"Tall friend?" Suzie said. "You mean Isabel? Long brown hair and lots of make-up?" The girl nodded. "Why would I want that?" The girls eyes did not meet with Suzie's, she was hiding something. *"Chérie,* why would I want that?" The frightened girl fled.

*

There was no sign of the carpet man over the next few days. Suzie was worried about Cactus Girl but as Carpet Man was nowhere to be seen, there was no sign of her either. Eric had summoned Suzie to the HQ boardroom that morning and she arrived happy, if a little flustered with the heat. As she stepped into the boardroom who should be sitting there in front of her but Carpet Man! Suzie's mouth fell open. Eric went to make the introductions, but Carpet Man got there first.

"Thank you, Erique... but we know each other already... do we not?" Suzie nodded.

"In that case Suzie you will already know that Mr Abdullah is one of Isabel's great finds. Marvellous! Shall we start?" One of the regional managers described how Carpet Man had set up some kind of co-operative with his business associates and was now asking the ad agency whether they and her shop would want to be part of it. They were eager, Suzie could see that, as it would mean lots of new business. It became clear that she had been asked there as the shop would be part of it all, and Suzie realised that senior management were pushing Carpet Man to take a leading role. However, the carpet man insisted that he would work best as a local advisor for them. The meeting ended with the agency as part of this collective and Carpet Man signed up as their new advisor. Plenty of handshakes followed.

Suzie just had time to search out a prize-winning pastry in the café before returning back to the shop. She caught sight of Isabel in her sunlit office. "What's all this about Mr Abdullah being one of your great finds, Isabel?"

"Well, someone had to do it. I had to make it right before he sucked you in completely. He's rude, obnoxious..."

"What are you talking about? This is the *carpet man* you are talking about, isn't it?"

"Oh, wake up, Suzie," Isabel snarled. "He was only ever priming you to further his own business options, can't you see that? Word on the street is that everyone here knows he's been wanting to come and work with us for years now. At least this way it's all above board. I've done you a favour. Bet you anything he's not interested in you now. You won't see him for dust." What had Isabel ever known about 'the word on the street'? She had always been too busy painting her nails to notice before. Isabel could be so hateful sometimes.

This month was full of surprises, first Christine's visit, then Carpet Man in the boardroom. Imagine Suzie's surprise when her own mother and sister dropped in unannounced at the flat two days later!

"Why have you not painted this flat yet, dear?"

"Wow… er… Hello, Mum. I guess I'll put my sister in the spare room…"

Mum walked into the flat.

"But it's so shabby, dear…"

"…and you can have Isabel's old room…"

"Paint isn't that expensive… I can see why Isabel moved out. Her flat is *much* nicer."

"Hang on…" Suzie started, "how do you know what her flat looks like when even I haven't seen that yet?"

"Photos, dear, photos." Suzie's mother flapped her hands disdainfully. Suzie bit back the obvious retort to go tell her to go stay at Isabel's if it was so shabby here.

The evening was no better. Her mother and sister spent the whole time refuting all of her successes or attributing them to Isabel in some way.

"As for your sales success… well… I'm sorry, dear… but do you think we were all born yesterday? No wonder your boyfriend has a new girl." What? Had they come all this way just to tell her that a 'substitute Suzie' was now living in her own UK flat? Was it their perverted way of easing the pain, or twisting the knife? She clearly had to sort out her flat back home now. If her boyfriend living there with a new floozy…

"Do you actually *know* all this?" Suzie demanded.

"Well… it's obvious, dear. When he realised you were not coming back just yet… By the way, you really should have told him yourself… it was the obvious thing to do. He is looking happier now than he has done for months so he *must* have a new girl."

Suzie had ignored her boyfriend's texts saying, *Come home immediately*, and just attributed these to his usual sullen rantings. He had obviously realised that the job was going to be longer than she stated and was not very pleased. When his texts went on and on she just replied, *why should I?* There had been radio silence ever since.

Her head pounded and her heart beat faster. With a rush of blood, Suzie could hear the music from 'Ride of the Valkyries' filling her head. She knew right then and there that she would show the whole darn lot of them. She would go and apply for Morocco's hit business series on TV. She had been joking about this with Isabel a couple of days ago. The drone of disdainful moaning continued in the background, so Suzie forgot momentarily that Isabel had not yet sent photos of her new flat to Suzie yet. She picked up her phone and texted her. *Get me the application form, quick!*

Isabel responded immediately. *Will do. You deserve it. I'll meet you in our favourite café tomorrow.* The deed was done.

Chapter 9

The Worm That Turned

The two girls met in the café at lunch as planned. As Isabel put sugar into her coffee Suzie looked at her with admiration. She had a way with people that seemed to charm them. She was like a well-oiled machine in the boardroom and had a kind of eloquence and focus in her speech that really teased out issues for discussion. Suzie had often tried to be as direct with people as Isabel was in meetings but instead was met with a completely different response. She had never completely worked out why. She did not begrudge her that, Isabel was undeniably good in the boardroom, which is where she supposed it counted most.

Suzie decided she would have to learn to be better in meetings and so mapped out a plan of action on a napkin. The two girls poured over this as they sipped their coffees.

"So, you are really going to do this? Apply for the TV series?" Isabel stirred her cup vigorously.

Suzie nodded. "I figure I can really learn to stand up for myself in the boardroom – if nothing else."

"It would certainly do that!" Isabel said with feeling. She paused to sip her coffee and then said, "Okay, I will help you with the application form and business plan, if you like."

"Oh, would you? Thanks!"

Isabel was a good friend. A little inscrutable sometimes, but a good friend.

*

Over the next week, Suzie thought carefully over her business idea. She costed it out so that she would at least have something to discuss when she and Isabel got together later that week. She started looking into courier services but could not decide on the best one. She had to look at the scope of her potential business idea – the size of the potential market – but she had not done that yet. If she truly wanted to do this she would have to figure out a way to provide cover at the print shop, and she would have to tell Eric. Oh boy. Tell Eric. Now that would be fun.

There was no way she would tell her mum or sister as she knew what they would say. They would tell her how much she was 'not up to the job', but if she didn't then apply as a result they would make her out to be a coward. She couldn't win either way, there was no pleasing them. Yes. Best not to say anything. Not just yet.

The weather had been truly dreadful in the UK this past week and she wondered how Mum was faring. CNN had said that parts of the UK were underwater. It seemed a world away. There was nothing but clear blue skies and beautiful sunsets here. She felt a tinge of guilt and hoped that everything was okay. She dialled the number.

"Mum? How are you?"

"Dreadful, dear, dreadful."

"What's up?"

"Well, whilst you are off sunning yourself in Morocco and your sister's off sunning herself on her cruise, spare a thought for the rest of us here. The whole place is underwater in the town. I have a leak in the roof, and the roofers can't come for another week! Buckets everywhere! Then next door's cat got into the loft, fell into the water tank, and drowned!" Suzie wished she hadn't asked. Mum continued, "How am I supposed to get a dead cat out of my water tank? And how am I supposed to clean it out? I have no idea how long it will be before I can drink that water again… I'm having to drink bottled water… Have you any idea how expensive bottled water is these days?" Mums voice drifted off as Suzie's mind went into autopilot and her eyes glazed over. No change there then. Mum was happy as ever. No point in saying anything, Mum never listened anyway. Mum's rant same to an end. "And of course nobody can get out and about as nobody wants to swim in water that is full of goodness knows what."

"Sorry to hear that." Suzie sighed. "I'll call next week. Hopefully things will be better by then." Mum was used to having her two girls around, but now she was having to cope with all this herself. Who *would* you call to sterilise your house's water tank? She didn't know. It had never been a subject that had come up before.

Suzie had had enough of CNN and flicked over the channel. Now showing was an animated film entitled *The*

Worm That Turned, which seemed to be about a group of fictional talking worms that lived in a community. One of the worms was always putting the others in danger without any thought for anyone else. There was a moral in there somewhere that struck a chord with Suzie, but she couldn't quite put her finger on what it was.

Today, Isabel was going to help her with the application and, quite sensitively for Isabel, they had agreed to meet in their favourite café to talk over Suzie's plans to apply for the Moroccan TV business series in more detail. As usual, Suzie was there first. She ordered a coffee and sat at one of the empty wooden tables at the side. The two side walls of the café were covered with mirrors that had filigree engravings around the outside of their borders. There was a pleasant hum of activity and clink of coffee cups as she waited.

"Ah, there you are," Isabel said as she flopped down on the chair opposite Suzie. Isabel clicked her fingers at the staff behind the counter who looked bemused. After a further disdainful click, the counter staff came forward and she ordered a drink. "So… come on, Suzie… what's your plan? How are you going to wow them?" she asked.

"I thought I would do a 'quick response printing business' but start with some stats about why it is needed."

"No need to do that," said Isabel, jotting something down.

"Oh…"

"No, personally I would just enter straight into what you are doing."

"Oh… okay… but I thought they needed the why and wherefores?"

"Yes, but if your idea is good enough it won't need explanation, will it?"

"I suppose not…"

"What about your sales plan?" Isabel asked excitedly. "You will need one of them."

"I thought I would use whatever means I can to get the printing to customers quickly."

"You will need a more concrete idea than that." Isabel was right.

"Come on… how many staff will you need? What distribution and stock levels will you need? Or are you planning just to 'schmooze' them in the boardroom?" Hmmm. Isabel knew full well how bad Suzie was at 'schmoozing'. It was probably her way of getting Suzie to think outside the box.

The two girls poured over ideas for the next hour until Suzie had a rough outline of what she was going to do for her business idea.

"We can finalise your plans later. I've printed out the form for you to apply for the TV series. They want to do it the old-fashioned way, paper copies posted, no e-mail applications. I'm just off to powder my nose." Isabel disappeared through the door labelled '*Toilettes*'.

Suzie mused over her plans. It could work. She was getting on at the shop much better now. A sudden noise in the café made her look up and she caught a look at herself in the side mirrors. Her blonde curly hair was all over the place – a ragged bird's nest. Her florid complexion was hardly the appearance that a business titan would want. The combination of being overweight and her overtight pink suit made her look like an overstuffed pig. Who was she kidding? She would have to smarten up.

Isabel's bag was balanced half on the chair and half not. One half suddenly tipped, and the weight of the bag caused it to crash to the floor. Suzie bent down quickly to pick it up. But there, peeking out of the bag, were *two* application forms for the TV business series! One had Isabel's name on it. Suzie quickly placed it back on the chair. The devious cow! Isabel was going to apply too, so why hide it? Why had she not mentioned this in all of their discussions today?

Chapter 10

Business Lesson Number Three

Suzie hardly had any time to wonder if Isabel planned to 'come clean' about applying to the TV series, as she was already late for 'business lesson number three'. Carpet Man met her at the edge of the souk after Isabel went her way.

"Look," he said, waving his arm at the stalls in front of them. "What do you see and hear?"

"I see a market full of people trying to get their shopping done."

"Ah, you see with Western eyes. Look again."

Suzie squinted in the sunlight. "Sorry, I can still only see people shopping. Not sure what you mean."

He pointed. "See that man? He is speaking to the customer in the man's ancient dialect. This respects the old gentleman's upbringing and brings happiness to his purchase. And look here…" he pointed to a man in a white turban and brown robes, "…he laughs and plays with the young boy who wants to buy the toy…" Suzie followed his gaze and noted that the man had a small palm-sized rag doll in the shape of a horse. He was pretending to make it canter around the rim of a nearby basket. "So, what is business lesson number three, Berber Girl?"

"Be respectful to your customers and talk to them how they would want to be spoken to."

"Good! Good."

*

Time passed pleasantly during the next few weeks. A natural friendship started to form between Suzie and the carpet man, and once a week he would take Suzie to sample some of the local cuisine and tell her more about the local way of life.

Today, they were meeting again for her next business lesson, and Carpet Man had invited her to sample Moroccan breakfast. Having followed his directions, she found the café and went inside. It had a small, well-used but meticulously clean serving bar at the back of the shop, and a few wooden tables and chairs in front of this. Almost all the seats were taken already despite this unearthly hour, but she spotted Carpet Man sitting in the corner. He pushed towards her what looked like golden balls of batter as she sat down. "*Sfenj*," he said. "They are made in three types: plain, with sugar, or with honey. Everyone eats these for breakfast in this region... Arabs, Berbers, Bedouins... everyone," he said, gesturing at the rest of the café's inhabitants. They were all men. She did not say anything. "They make these only in the morning. Some people eat them in the afternoon, but they are best eaten fresh. Try some." He picked up one of them, tilted his head backwards, and put one whole ball into his mouth. Suzie followed suit. As she did so, she noticed the eyes of the men on the surrounding tables watching her. *Sfenj* were a kind of spongey doughnut which went really well with the mint tea that was poured from a great height. "Which do you like best?" he asked.

"The ones with honey I think." This seemed to please him.

"Ah, you are a true Berber girl, yes?"

Suzie laughed. As they ate he explained that he was a Berber and that his people were indigenous to the local area, and in the whole of North Africa. He told her of the ancient Berber languages, how they were mostly spoken languages and how all Moroccans came to speak French. He told her about all the Berber factions in the Maghreb region and the differences between them. Suzie had no idea that there were Berber subdivisions. The carpet man looked sad when he described the way some Berbers no longer spoke their traditional language, and how this was now limited to a few of the older generation like himself. "To be Berber is not just eating certain foods, speaking a certain language, or living in a certain way," he said. "We are a noble people. We call ourselves '*i-Mazigh-en*' and think of ourselves as free people, although sadly we are not so free these days."

"What do you mean?" Suzie asked, draining her cup of mint tea.

"There are those who do not allow us to refer to our children by their proper Berber names, but that is for another time, yes? Now… we both need to get ready for work." Suzie looked at her watch, it was gone 7am.

"Yes, you're right." Suzie stood and pushed her chair back. "Many thanks for breakfast. Business lesson number four was learning about the culture you are doing business in, am I right?"

Carpet Man nodded his head and exited the shop. "Next time I take you for Arab breakfast."

"Okay, you're on," she said as they parted company.

*

Carpet Man was as good as his word. Although he did not usually work Saturdays he appeared two days later at 11am and sat patiently waiting opposite Suzie's flat. She waved, jumped up and went down to meet him. He led her through saffron-coloured alleys to an area she had not seen before. Old men were sitting around on benches smoking, eating, and talking. One of them was smoking one of the large bubbling smoking pipes in a corner. "Don't sit out here," he said as Suzie went to find a seat. "You will need to follow me and come inside." She obeyed as it seemed to be important to him. Inside was a similar set up to the *sfenj* shop (as she was now calling it). It had the same type of serving bar with men behind, and wooden tables and chairs in front. She heard him order what sounded like *mawah* and ten minutes later the food arrived with a pot of steaming coffee. "This is Arab bread," he said. "They call it *msemen* and pronounce it 'me-samen'. '*Me*' means 'with', and '*samen*' means 'clarified butter'."

"Oh… like Indian ghee?" Suzie asked.

"Exactly. We Berbers call it *malawah*. To you English, it is bread and butter," he said with a twinkle in his eye. "Try some."

She took a piece. It was like no bread and butter she had ever tasted. It was more like a yeasted pancake. Some bits were a little dry and bland, and others a little soggy. The soggy bits felt flaccid in the mouth and not particularly nice. "What's in it?" she enquired.

"Flour, semolina, yeast, butter, salt, sugar, and water to make the dough. Arabs come and eat here for 'elevenses'." Carpet Man's eyes twinkled again.

"Sorry... but I think I prefer *sfenj*."

"Ha!" he said. "Definitely a proper Berber girl, no?" They both laughed.

From this point onwards Carpet Man had taken to calling her Berber Girl, and they continued to meet in various places to explore the local cuisine and discuss Moroccan culture – despite the ferociously hot weather. Not once had Suzie asked him what his real name was as she knew from the co-operative meeting that day at HQ that it was Mr Abdullah.

*

In the days that followed Suzie tried to visit the first shop again to buy some *sfenj* but was just met with perplexed-looking faces behind the counter. Granted, she had limited French, but they seemed to think it strange that she should come in and ask – especially as she wanted to take them away and not eat them then and there.

Isabel made fun of her little food outings and was

really insulting, calling the food 'foreign muck'. She had even asked if Suzie had a thing going with the carpet man.

"Don't be ridiculous! And don't be so offensive!" Suzie said indignantly. "I am just learning about the culture, just as Eric asked us to do."

"Keep telling yourself that, baby girl," Isabel retorted. "You can't seriously be going just for the free food. I mean... Moroccan food is all intestines, omelette sandwiches, and that disgusting 'eggy' tomato dish. So, if you are not going for the food, it must be something else."

*

Gradually over these weeks when they met up, Suzie had realised that Carpet Man lived and performed a lot of his business in the actual desert. "Don't you find it a difficult existence?" she had asked him at their last meeting. She expected him to say 'yes' but he didn't. He explained how much he loved the desert and 'how it talked to him'. Seeing her bemused face he explained that in one way it is like any other landscape. When you are familiar with it you know how to 'read it'. He gave her an example of seeing a hooded lad, hands in pockets, walking up and down the streets in London. "As a female alone, would you ask him where to go if you were lost?"

"No, if I was lost I would probably find an old lady to ask."

"You see, you have made a choice about what is in front of you. You read the signs. It is the same with the desert. You see a sandstorm approaching? You don't go that way. You have a long journey? You make a stop on the way where you know you will find water at all times of the year. You want to travel but it is midday and the sun is at its highest? You don't travel at that time." He paused. "It is not so hard... the desert is kind to you when you have known it as long as I have. Me and my ancestors have been talking with the desert for many generations." He had eyed Suzie carefully. He could see she was thinking hard about what he had said. "Come with me one day, I will show you."

Suzie smiled. "I very much look forward to that. Thank you." She was curious. He did have great eyes but no, she definitely did *not* have a 'thing going' with the carpet man.

Chapter 11

The Agafay Desert

The following Friday, the carpet man came to find her after work at her flat. "You come with us tomorrow?" he enquired. "You come to the desert? I will teach you." She didn't have much planned, just a bit of shopping with Isabel which could go on hold, so she agreed.

"What should I wear?" It was a genuine question; she had never dressed for the desert before, and city temperatures were in way up in the thirties. She guessed it would be even hotter in the desert as there would be no buildings to provide shade.

"Wear good, flat, covered shoes... sunglasses... a scarf, and trousers light in colour... and bring lots of water." He winked at Suzie as if to say, 'You English like your water'. They made arrangements to meet at the old clocktower which was actually not a clocktower at all but where all of the local Arab men spent a lot of time discussing the finer points of life. Suzie had heard (from the limited bits of Arabic language she had picked up since her arrival) that it had apparently gained its nickname as you could hear 'What time is it?' at pretty much any time of the day there.

*

On arrival at the clocktower the next day she noted that locals asking each other the time was pointless as none of them could answer. None of them seemed to have watches! If any of them eventually gained an answer to this question, they never seemed to get up, make apologies, or move elsewhere. It was all very odd.

The carpet man appeared. "Come! I show you where we get camels."

Camels? Suzie thought. *Oh, it's the desert. Of course there would be camels, duh!* They wound their way to the outskirts of the city where a Jeep was waiting for them. "Camels, eh? You really had me going there, Car..." she began, but aware of a band of men that seemed to be with Carpet Man watching her, she corrected herself, "I mean, Mr Abdullah."

"Ah, you thought we were going to *this* desert?" he motioned with his hand towards the desert stretched in front of them. "No, this is not very interesting, just stony and dry. I am going to show you the *proper* desert. My home, the Agafay desert."

Suzie hopped into the Jeep which soon stopped temporarily outside a small carpet warehouse that Suzie assumed belonged to the carpet man. Fifteen minutes later the Jeep came to a halt and she clambered out. The first thing that struck her was the sheer 'orangeness' of the sand, earth, and rocks in front of her. You think that it cannot possibly be that bright, deep orange that you see in photos, but it really was. Something about the colour conjured up images of men in turbans of purple and gold – like those in *Arabian Nights*. A further party of three men and seven camels stood waiting for them.

Carpet Man showed Suzie the best way to mount one of the camels (whose English equivalent name was 'Hazel'), then he mounted his own camel. "Don't worry, she will follow. There is nothing you need to do." Hazel behaved perfectly for a few minutes then, after making a few low and deep gurgling noises, craned her neck around and propelled a hard ball of camel spit right between Suzie's eyes. Charming! After a shaky start Suzie learnt how to stop Hazel doing this by digging her in the ribs with her feet. They were getting along much better now.

Carpet Man sidled up to Suzie's camel. "She likes you," he said, smiling. "It normally takes her two weeks to stop spitting at new people. Look, see. This is my washbasin." He spread his hands wide but Suzie could see nothing but sand. He jumped off his camel with an ease that belied his age and crouched to pick up what looked like a spiky, light-brown, but ultimately dead plant. He poured out water from his flask and added the dried plant leaves. It lathered up like washing up liquid. "Makes good shampoo too," he said.

Suzie was amazed. "Is your washbasin always here?"

Carpet Man laughed. "No! It is wherever the desert puts it next. It's like your English game of hide and seek."

"Seriously, though. How do you find your way in the desert? That has always mystified me."

"There are many ways... The stars, wind, moon... and even the way the sand falls sometimes. But you are missing the point. You don't always have to go looking for things you need in the desert, they often come and find you." He explained that in the Western world everything was immediate. "You dial a meal to be delivered, or you go to the supermarket and buy, cook, and eat. You want to eat in the desert? You have to catch or find it first! If you see a gazelle and you know it is still six hours before you will stop to eat, and you know that the place you are going has no food, what do you do? You kill the gazelle, rest the carcass over a camel, and drain its blood when you get there. You take food when you can."

"I see."

"In the Western world, the radio or TV tell you what the weather will be like. Here we look for ourselves: Blood-orange moon? Windy next day; brown sky on the horizon? Sandstorm coming. Even animals and plants tell us about the weather."

Was he trying to make her believe he was some kind of mystical Dr Dolittle or something? "How so?" she asked. He explained about 'red' tides for shellfish on the coast. Suzie was still doubtful.

"Your English salmon, how do they know when it is time to travel upstream? Your English birds," he continued. "How do they know to fly south for winter to find warmer climates? How do they know what trees to build their nests in?" Suzie had no idea but remembered her dad telling her when she was little that you can tell whether it will be a hot summer or harsh winter by how high up in the trees the birds made their nests. High up, the weather will be hot. Low down, the winter will be harsh. It made sense. This was not enigmatic mysticism; it was just the carpet man's finely honed observation skills and years of practice. "Come, we have several more miles before I show you my oasis."

Being a camel novice, Suzie had no idea how tiring or 'gritty' camel travel could be. The slight breeze would pick up stray grains of sand and dance and play with them. At first the tickle of sand grains brushing against her cheek was not unpleasant, but after a couple of hours this became chaffing to the skin. She noted that the men had all taken a part of their turbans down and wrapped the loose end around their faces. She followed suit with her scarf. Roll on that oasis!

Twenty minutes later a 'watering hole' appeared complete with a flat-roofed café and a gas-fuelled barbeque! Carpet Man tied up the camels and stood talking to his companions. She went inside. To her astonishment there was not just electricity but a flat-screen TV with football blaring out. The TV looked out of context – the walls were shabby, the toilets were holes in the ground, and the seats were wooden banquettes scattered with worn-looking cushions. Carpet Man noticed Suzie staring and smiled. "Commercialisation – what can you do?" He shrugged, picked up the beer his companions had ordered for him, and sat himself down.

Suzie followed suit. "I didn't imagine there would be anything like this here. I suppose this is a bit like an oasis if you are really thirsty…"

"This?" He laughed. "No. This is not the oasis. Like I said, you use what the desert puts in front of you. Right now, it has put this cold beer in front of me…"

An hour or so later, with a light lunch inside them, Suzie

realised that the carpet man had expertly timed the break to avoid the worst of the day's sun. As they readied the camels the carpet man's travel companions nodded to her, but so far they had not spoken to her directly.

"How is it that you talk to me but the others don't?" she asked.

"I have told them you are my Western business associate who is interested in doing business with us in the desert. They respect the business ethic. Most of them do not understand Western ways or a Western woman's thinking. If I said that you were interested in the Berber way of life they would not have let you come. Women don't observe such things here."

"I understand. Thank you."

After a further camel trudge of ten minutes, Carpet Man stopped the camel procession momentarily to shout something to the guys at the rear of the line. Two men peeled off and headed away with the spare camel trailing behind. The rest of the afternoon was spent peacefully gliding over the tops of the dunes with Carpet Man pointing out plants and points of interest along the way. Around 5pm he announced that they would soon arrive at the oasis. Suzie could see nothing but sand in all directions. "You wait," he said. "You'll see."

Suzie thought she was starting to suffer from heat stroke because there in the middle of nowhere she thought she saw an area of shrubs and palm trees. She did! It was real! It had been completely hidden by the last dune. It even had a stretch of water which Carpet Man said was fed by an underground spring, and a large tree with what looked like black specs all over it.

"My bank account," Carpet Man said.

"The tree?" Suzie queried. "Your bank account?" As they got closer she could see that the black specs were actually goats! She had never seen anything like this in her whole life.

"My savings account," Carpet Man continued, eyes twinkling. He explained that when he needed more money he just sold one of his tree-climbing goats. She then noticed that the two men that had peeled off their group earlier were here and had set up camp. They were busy spit-roasting 'meaty chunks' of something. Probably a gazelle. They were jeering good humouredly at Suzie and Carpet Man. She supposed that she looked a little weird in several layers in this heat, but they were to protect her fair skin from the sun. She could not understand the language they used but it was clear they were now saying "What took you so long?". The men around Suzie pointed at her. She responded by raising her eyebrows in a 'What? Who me?' type way, but then nodded. They found this to be hilarious for some reason and fell about laughing.

The light was beginning to fade by the time they had finished their meal and set off again, so Suzie was becoming a little worried. She knew that Carpet Man would get her back safely, but it would take hours in the dark. It had to be a long way back because they had been travelling all day.

However, a little later and not for the first time that day, Suzie was completely astonished. As they rounded a large dune the city came into view! How was this even possible? Carpet Man must have taken her around in a complete circle!

Wearily she said goodbye to Hazel and clambered into the Jeep that was waiting for them. Carpet Man said something to the driver, so he took them all to her flat door. Suzie climbed out, waved goodbye to the carpet man and his men, put her sandy clothes in the linen basket, and jumped into the shower.

As she was drying her hair, her mobile phone dinged. It was Isabel. *Fancy coming out for meal tonight?* the text said.

Suzie quickly thumbed a message: *Thanks, but I'm strictly a 'one gazelle a day' type girl. Let's do a raincheck.*

Chapter 12

Summoned Home

"Ah... this is the life." Suzie sat on her balcony looking out over the city with her feet up and sipped a mug of steaming mint tea. It was 6am on Monday and Suzie wrapped an oversized cardigan more closely around her against the slight morning chill. 6am was one of the only times that Marrakesh was quiet and still.

At 6.30am the obligatory call to prayer started drifting across the still morning air. This was Suzie's alarm call to tell her that her daily balcony time would soon give way to hurried work preparations. She padded into the kitchen to warm a couple of croissants through and soon the smell of coffee filled the flat. Just enough time for one last cuppa. The day had begun.

As she walked to work she watched the town slowly stir into life. Men started to load carts, and the odd motorcycle zoomed past. The saffron walls turned to a deep-terracotta colour, signalling that she had one last square to cross before reaching the shop. The smallest of breezes was now dancing around her. She felt alive. She had not felt like this for a very long time.

Sadly, her exhilaration was short-lived because as soon as she entered the shop, Hassan (the deputy shop manager-cum-photographic incumbent) told her that the main office wanted her to call them as soon as she got in that morning. It transpired that she had been called back to the UK for an important meeting with a large UK advertising company. She was to be on a plane the day after tomorrow. Groaning inwardly, she checked the flights and shot off a quick e-mail to confirm she would be there. Her old UK boss fired back an equally quick e-mail saying, *Good, I'll square it with Eric. I thought you'd be pleased.* Nothing was further from the truth. She supposed she would have to face her boyfriend now as it had been four months since she had left, and she had hinted but never really told him exactly when she was coming back. This time was as good as any. He had probably realised their relationship was over by now anyway, hence the rumours via Mum of the new girlfriend.

Andy arrived later that morning with the latest set of prints for Suzie's first local ad campaign. They were brilliant as usual. She explained that he would have to go ahead without her for the second part of the photographic plan as she had been called back to the UK for a few days. "Great! Free reign at last!" he said with a grin on his face.

"No. No free reign. Just stick to the plan, or I won't pay you!" Suzie retorted. Andy stuck his bottom lip out in mock sadness. Suzie laughed and pointed to the shop door. "Go! Before I have to chase you out!"

Andy grinned again, like a naughty schoolboy. "I'm going, I'm going!"

The shop was quiet once more. The day passed quickly and Suzie spent an uninterrupted afternoon deciding which prints would be used for the ad posters.

*

Back at the flat later that day she spread all of the items needed for the London trip out on her bed. She used to spend hours deciding what skirt went with what top before packing cases, but today she was done in half an hour. "That'll do," she said, squashing the case flat.

*

On the day in question, she took an early morning taxi to the airport. The walk to the terminal and queue for boarding had seemed long, but the baby crying in the seat behind her during the flight seemed *interminably* long. Sporting a fixed and frozen look on her face, Suzie stood waiting for her baggage. As expected, 'boyfriend' was not there to meet her even though she had texted him about her return.

As Suzie turned the key in the lock of her flat, she was surprised to see her mum waiting inside. "Mum! What are you doing here? Wasn't expecting you…"

"Nice way to greet your mother, dear."

"Sorry, just surprised that's all. You didn't mention it in your text."

"Well, we have been looking after your flat for you since your boyfriend left," Mum replied.

"What? He left? How long ago was that?"

"Oh a few weeks ago." Mum flapped her hands. "I personally don't blame him."

Suzie had assumed he would be living there most of the time whilst she was away, as she always had done, but of course he would have left it. He had his own flat and she had after all been away a while now. Suzie didn't comment on her mum's last comment, but she was right. "Hang on," Suzie said. "How did you get a key?" Please God let them say he has given them his key.

"He had one cut for us."

So… somewhere a disenfranchised boyfriend… who is probably out of her life for good… is wandering around with keys to her empty flat. Great! She made a mental note to talk with him and get the locks changed whilst she was in the UK. Suzie then noticed that her sister was sitting in her favourite chair with her feet up on the coffee table, texting goodness knows who. "You could say thanks to Mum, Suzie," she grumbled but did not look up.

Suzie's mum seemed to be trying to make conversation. "How is the job going? I bet the boardroom is hard," Mum said. "They all go at each other like dogs, don't they."

"It's okay." Suzie shrugged. "They don't really have a boardroom where I am. In fact, I'm enjoying it." Life was often hard at work but she had no intention of telling Mum that.

Mum thrust a piece of what looked like marble cake under nose. "Here have this." Cake *and* politeness? These were not things Suzie usually associated with Mum. And then it came.

"Do you think you will stay in Morocco?" For the first

time Suzie's sister looked up from her phone. They probably expected her to say 'no', but she heard herself saying an emphatic 'yes' followed by a passionate explanation of how things were so much better there. "Well… just make sure you make the most of it while it lasts," Mum finished as she walked out the door. "Opportunities like these do not grow on trees, Suzanne, and loyal boyfriends don't either…" her voice trailed down the hall.

"Don't expect us to visit you there again," her sister said walking out the door. "It was crap…"

After a lifetime of disinterest about her career choices, and cross-examinations that the Spanish Inquisition would be proud of, she could not really have expected them to be supportive. "Yadda, yadda. Whatever." Suzie sighed and closed the door.

*

The meeting the next day went very smoothly. Suzie's new-found business confidence went down well with the large UK advertising company in the boardroom, and they agreed to collaborate on the next big ad campaign. Even her old boss looked pleased and had taken her out for a celebratory drink. Just as her old boss had set the drinks down, Suzie's phone rang. It was Christine. "Wasn't sure when was a good time to ring you as I know you are only here on a flying visit. We'd better meet up… there's some things you need to know."

"What? Tell me now!" Suzie said.

"No, hon. I'll meet you in the Old Duke just around the corner in thirty minutes when you're finished. Bye for now."

*

Suzie sat in the darkened pub and listened whilst Christine told her that she thought Suzie's boyfriend was having an affair.

"That's what my mum said and I didn't know whether to believe her or not. He may not be perfect but I didn't have him down as a philandering pig. Just insensitive sometimes," Suzie said. "Are you sure, Christine?"

"Well not totally sure, but the signs are there, hon, they really are."

"Like what?"

"Well… his indifference to what you are doing…"

"But he's always been like that…"

"Him not meeting you at the airport, him not being at the flat, him moving out of the flat a few weeks ago without telling you… Face it, hon, it all points to one thing."

"But wouldn't he let me know of he had ended the relationship?" Suzie cried.

"Not necessarily. Some guys don't these days. After all, did you? Did you tell him the truth about being in Morocco for six months, and did you tell him it was over between you?" She had a point. Suzie had taken this Morocco thing partly to shake her boyfriend into some kind of action, but when this backfired she had consoled herself with the fact that they at least loved each other. Or so she had thought. She had to agree it was over now; facts don't lie, but to leave her flat empty without a word *and* him having an affair too? It was a lot to take in.

She told Christine about how he had looked at her with stone-like eyes and said, 'If you go now, don't you dare come back to me,' and how she had snapped and said, 'I damn well won't then.'

"I know," Christine said. "You cried down the phone for a whole three hours. It's probably for the best, you know."

Suzie was quiet for a moment and sighed. "You are probably right."

"Really? Stop the press – major surprise! I thought you would kill me for saying that!"

"Well... he has not really spoken to me since I left... and it was on shaky ground months before that..."

"Look," Christine said. "I have some annual leave coming up in two weeks' time. How about I come to Morocco and be your personal support service?"

"It's not needed." Suzie laughed. "But it would be great to see you."

Suzie's mobile rang. It was Andy in Marrakesh. "Suzie, you got a minute?"

"Yes, what's up?"

"It's urgent," Andy said. She sighed. Christine mimed 'goodbye', motioned that she would ring Suzie, and left the pub. Andy's normally jovial voice sounded strained. "Ah, Suzie. Not good news I'm afraid. Sorry to call you but the deputy shop manager, Hassan, would not take my last set of prints."

"What?" Suzie exclaimed. "But they were your best yet."

"Well, he wouldn't take them... probably because you're not here, or he felt he could have done better himself."

She doubted that. "I will pay you anyway," she said.

89

"Any one of them would be perfect. How dare he? Wait 'til I get back, I will give him a piece of my mind…"

"I'm afraid that's not all the bad news."

"What?"

"He won't be there to receive a piece of your mind when you get back because he walked out late yesterday."

"Oh, man…" Suzie was silent for a moment or two. "But who is manning the shop? He's supposed to be in charge. Is it just you there?"

"Well… that's the problem… which is why I thought I had better ring you first. Nobody is. Sophia the casual girl is on annual leave, Ahmed is not confident enough to run the place yet and I don't know his contact details, and it seems that nobody has shop keys. Hassan locked up and took the keys with him."

"So… let me get this straight. Hassan's just shut up shop with a sign on the door saying 'Closed, will reopen soon' or something?"

"Not even that, it's just shut. I saw three other people waiting for quite a while with me this morning then they just walked away. That's why I thought I had better let you know what was going on."

Damn! She would have to get back to Morocco earlier than planned to sort this all out. "Sit tight, Andy. I will come back ASAP. In the meantime, I will square it with HQ to get you some keys. Can you put up a sign saying 'Trading as usual tomorrow' on the shop door? I will get someone from HQ to come over."

"I can do better than that," he said. "I can man the shop until you get back if you like?"

"Would you? How wonderful! I won't forget this you know!"

"You better hadn't. I'm still waiting for the money for my wasted photos, remember…"

Suzie was laughing with joy. "I'll pay double!"

"Could it be triple if I turn out to be a good manager?" Andy asked.

"Done!" she said. Crisis averted. Thank God for Andy.

She supposed she had better give 'boyfriend' a ring. She called him but, for the sake of peace decided to say nothing about him possibly having an affair, or the fact that it was probably over between them. She hated herself for this and would probably regret that decision. To her surprise, he answered.

"What do you want?"

"Nice way to say hello."

"Well… what do you expect." He had a point. She had, after all, just expected him to wait in the flat until she got back.

His petulant jibes still had an annoying way of softening her heart. Against her better judgement she found herself saying, "I am sure we can work out this long-distance relationship thing, but looks like Morocco will be a longer than I thought… Maybe we could get together whilst I am here in the UK?"

"What do you mean 'whilst' you are here? Your mum told me you were back for good! How long is it this time? And don't say four weeks…" Rumbled. "Anyway… I'm not around at the moment." His tone was blunt.

The dialling tone had sounded funny, as if he was abroad somewhere, but she ploughed on. "Yes, I guessed you were back at your flat. Would you mind keeping an eye on mine please? Sorry I haven't actually asked you yet about that. I thought that as you spent most of your time at mine you would just carry on doing that, my bad."

"But you weren't there, why would I?" Again, he had a point and she knew it. She should just come clean. But while she was contemplating this he spoke up. "Okay, I'll drop by from time to time if it's what you want… but I'm a bit busy at the moment."

She was not sure why he suddenly agreed but said nothing. "Thank you. I would feel better knowing that you were keeping an eye on the flat. Hey! Here's an idea… why don't you come out to Morocco with me? Have a bit of a free holiday?"

"No, no, *no!*" he said a little too vehemently. "Told you, I'm too busy at the moment."

"It was just a suggestion…" Suzie guessed he would take a while to come around to the idea she was going to be in Morocco for a bit longer. "Let's sort this all out properly when we next see each other, eh?"

"Uh… okay…" he said, and the line went dead.

Chapter 13

Business as Usual

After talking to her boyfriend, Suzie decided that if he really did have another woman he would have been much more defensive. As a result, she didn't really believe the rumours but felt sheepish and began to feel a little sorry for him. She therefore had no reason to get her flat locks changed which in turn meant she could return to Morocco without a second thought. She had managed to get her flight changed, so bright and early the next morning she was sitting on the plane back to Marrakesh. She hadn't really ever envisaged a jet-setting lifestyle before this, it was a lot more tiring and less glamorous than she had imagined. At least she knew the shop was in safe hands until she got back, so she could relax a bit.

Suzie absent-mindedly watched the floating clouds from the aeroplane window. She decided that she had been far too passive with her life up to now. She was allowing it to direct *her* instead of grabbing it by the scruff of the neck, beating it into submission, and shaping her future herself.

The man in front of her on the plane coughed and Suzie popped some crisps into her mouth. She was not exactly sure where she belonged now but she felt more at home in Morocco than she had ever done in the UK. After all, there was nothing to keep her in England now so she may as well sell her UK flat. Morocco was not a total bed of roses but it really felt like home. She licked the salt off her fingers. Somewhere at the back of the plane a stressed mother was berating her overtired children. The clouds on the other side of the plane seemed to have formed a solid cotton-wool blanket over the whole sky now except for a small ray of sunshine that was desperately trying to become a cloudburst.

She called over the flight attendant for a newspaper and spoke to him in Arabic with the few words she had picked up. He seemed charmed that she had made the effort to speak to him in his native language and gave her his best smile. She flicked open the newspaper and started reading for something to pass the time.

Oh look! It's one of our national ads! That looks so good!

Christine had texted Suzie around twenty bad jokes before she flew in an effort to keep Suzie's mind off the boyfriend dilemma. Suzie closed the paper and thumbed through these as she saw the UK come into view through the small plane window.

By 12.30pm she was at her shop with luggage in tow. Nothing major or further untoward had happened and Andy was doing a brilliant job. She confirmed with Andy whether he was free to cover the afternoon for her as she had to get over to HQ for a meeting. He said yes.

She wrestled a few items out of the luggage, left the bags under the counter, and promised that she would be back to collect them before the shop closed. She just had time to freshen up after the flight and get a bit of lunch before the meeting.

Grabbing a can of Coke and tub of falafels from the nearest food shop, Suzie decided to catch some rays and headed for the central gardens to eat her lunch. She also wanted to try out a new sunscreen she had picked up from the airport. 'In no time at all you will turn a delicious shade of brown' it boasted. 'Suitable for all skin types'. Suzie settled herself beneath a large cactus and sat down on the flat rock that had been fashioned into a seat. She slapped on the lotion liberally and flipped open the Kindle app on her phone as she wanted to read the latest novel a woman on the plane had recommended to her.

On arrival at HQ thirty minutes later, Suzie felt surprisingly rested after her flight. With a flurry of brown curls and a wave of Calvin Klein's latest perfume Isabel raced up to her. "You are not going into the meeting like that are you? What have you done to your face?"

"What?"

"Oh really! Hobson's office in ten, and don't be late." Isabel's brown curls bounced off and she was gone.

Suzie scooted off to the women's loo to see what Isabel was talking about. Damn! The wondrous sun lotion had made her face go a bright shade of orange! It obviously contained some self-tanning product but this was now mixed with sunburn, and the mixture of the two was steadily producing a bright shade of orangey-red. Suzie searched around her handbag for some kind of foundation to address the situation. Katy, a colleague from the next office, came in and saw what she was doing.

"No, no. That stuff won't do it. You need a bit of natural-looking coverage. Here, try this." She thrust a compact of multicoloured-looking stuff into Suzie's hands. "Go on," she urged. With three deft swipes from her enormous brush, the magical powder had hidden the 'sunburnt satsuma' look and transformed it into a beautiful sun-kissed glow. Suzie topped it up with some eyeliner and a touch of lippy from her bag.

"I gotta get me some *that*!" Suzie said, delighted. "What is it?"

Much to Isabel's apparent annoyance, the meeting with Hobson went very well. Suzie's calm and relaxed attitude had spilled over from the lunch break into the boardroom, and her new 'make-up inspired confidence' seemed to impress Hobson. Isabel's face was like thunder later on when Eric their line manager announced that both she and Suzie also would be taking on the large Donovan account.

"I thought you would be pleased to work together." Eric smiled. After exiting the office Isabel was not amused.

"What's wrong, Isabel? I can see there is something." Isabel assured Suzie it was nothing to do with her, the work, or the meeting, but it was all about her brother. Suzie was shocked as she didn't even know Isabel had a brother. She had never mentioned him before. Suzie surveyed her face. Isabel did look genuinely worried but refused to say any more. Suzie decided to get her a cuppa and a plate of her favourite cookies. Bingo! Isabel's smile was back. Isabel was a funny person at times.

Before she left for the day, Suzie got the name of the magical foundation Katie had let her use earlier. Within a week she ordered a six-month supply of 'Glo-time mineral foundation' compacts and had perfected that 'immaculate unblemished skin' look that Suzie had coveted for so many years. Alas, Katy had had no such miracle ideas to tame her unruly hair. Pity.

*

Andy had been as good as he had promised and had kept the shop going during her absence. During the following few days, he took on more and more of the managerial roles under Suzie's direction and was a complete godsend. There had been only three negative events in the shop.

With Andy's presence, the shop staff were at least nodding to her when they left the shop for a smoke or coffee break. She had noticed that they now no longer took more than the allotted time for breaks and wondered whether Andy or the carpet man had had a quite word with them during her absence. Or perhaps the fact that she had learnt a lot about Moroccan ways and Berber values had not gone unnoticed by the staff?

Chapter 14

What Is Going On?

Today, Suzie was heading up to HQ for the 9am meeting and got there early as usual, but there was definitely a feeling of uneasiness in the office. Or was she imagining it? She used to feel like this most of the time back in the UK but things were usually so different here. Carpet Man had taught her to trust her own instincts. Yes… a feeling of uneasiness definitely hung in the air like a leaden cloud, and it seemed to revolve around her for some reason. Nobody actually said anything but things were slightly strained. Why? Some colleagues gave half-smiles through gritted teeth and in the past she had often put this sort of thing down to her own insecurities and paranoia. This time she knew it was real.

"What's going on?" Suzie asked Tony.

"What do you mean?"

"You know… the heavy atmosphere…"

"Oh… there has been a lot of stress here recently. You know… account irregularities… stock missing… By the way, where's Isabel?" Tony asked.

"On her way, I suppose," Suzie replied. "I wouldn't know, I haven't shared the flat with her for a while."

"Oh... I didn't know that." He was quiet for a moment. "I wonder about that girl sometimes." He made his way over to the coffee 'pod', jiggling his empty coffee cup loosely between his thumb and forefinger as he went.

Isabel had a gift for making you think that you knew everything about her so it had taken Suzie a long time to realise that Isabel never usually talked about her past or her family. Only last week a guy in the HQ office had asked Suzie what Isabel's favourite colour was as he wanted to buy her some flowers. She had to admit she had no idea, and that's how it started. Suzie got to wondering about other things and had always comforted herself that Isabel would never do anything untoward, as she was charming and effervescent and knew exactly what to say to quickly put Suzie's mind at rest. She then had the uneasy realisation for the first time that she actually knew very little about Isabel. What else did Isabel have to hide? She had certainly seen a different side to her lately that she kept mostly hidden from others. Nobody else except Tony seemed to notice though. That was just it, when you doubted her you always somehow followed that up with excusing her and ultimately doubting yourself. Suzie knew that things were not quite right so maybe Isabel did have a brother that she was worried about? She just couldn't put her finger on what was going on somehow.

Isabel blew in ten minutes later sporting a beautiful turquoise scarf that billowed and fluttered behind her as she moved. Her brown curls cascaded down her back. It gave the overall impression that she was gracefully floating around the office. Her mood was slightly cool, which she said was the result of a raucous party the evening before, but a couple of double espressos later she was back to her usual bubbly self.

"Hey," she said. "Have you got your TV series application back yet?"

"No. Not yet," Suzie said.

"Ah. I have. I'm sure they will get around to sending you yours soon," Isabel soothed.

So, Isabel finally admitted she had entered. Great. This probably meant Suzie had not met the required standard.

"When do they start?"

"Well filming for the series starts in three weeks but I have to do some pieces to camera before that."

"Congratulations, Isabel. I'm sure you will dazzle them." Suzie sighed.

*

When the TV series e-mail came it was short but informative. Suzie was overjoyed. It asked her to come to the palace as they were going to shoot the 'bio' bits there. There were a few guidelines on how to present the business you wanted to pitch to Farid Burhan – who was Morocco's answer to Sir Alan Sugar, and a section on what to bring with you. "I gotta get me a haircut." Suzie sighed. "Maybe I'll try that one in the centre of town." She had been recommended a hairdressers, and an Italian guy there named Antonio in particular.

Antonio had spikey hair that was fashionably untidy. It gave him an air of sophisticated coolness that many would find difficult to carry off. He warmly welcomed her in and sat her down. She explained that she was going to appear on TV and he seemed to know exactly what she needed. He then started cutting and OMG! Instead of gently cutting the hair and letting it fall to the ground like all other hairdressers, Antonio was flinging the cut hair upwards at a frightening rate of knots. It was like watching the Muppet's Swedish chef at work. The result, however, was perfection... a miracle! In less than twenty minutes she had been transformed from 'female docker' to 'doyenne'. Wow! She asked him if he could turn her from 'frump' to 'fashion icon' in one easy move and he laughed.

"You like it, eh?"

"I love it! Nobody has ever been able to tame my curls before."

"Anti-frizz shampoo... and argan oil... that is the secret," he added conspiratorially. "I can put a bottle in your bag to take home if you like?" There was a faint sheen of perspiration on his face.

"Please do. You are a lifesaver!"

*

Suzie had been dreading the moment she told Eric that she would be needing a couple of week's annual leave so that she could attend the Morocco's top business series, but he was surprisingly supportive.

"Look, if you need more than two weeks I'm sure we can manage. Andy is doing great at the shop, and Ahmed is coming along nicely."

Suzie was suspicious. "Are you sure?"

"Absolutely. As I said, we positively encourage this. Farid would be a great collaborator for this company." Suzie looked at him in disbelief. He continued, "Didn't Isabel tell you that? I thought she would have done so when she suggested you both enter, you both being friends and all."

"No, she didn't mention it. And applying was not her idea," she managed to blurt out. *Friends indeed*, thought Suzie. *So, Isabel had said this was all her idea, eh?*

"No matter. Just let me know if you need a little longer."

"I doubt I will get past the first task, but yes, I will definitely let you know," Suzie said. Eric being nice to her? What was going on?

*

Carpet Man noticed Suzie looking glum the next morning as she stepped out to work. She confessed that she did not know what to do about her boyfriend.

"Ah. Young love. Always so inscrutable. Does he love you?"

"I'm not sure."

"Does he come to see you?"

"No."

"Does he call you?"

"No."

"Then he does not love you. Perhaps you should go for older men?"

Suzie looked at him quizzically, and Carpet Man maintained eye contact. Was he flirting with her? She

looked away. "Sorry, I have to go to work. See you later."
What was going on?

At work she decided to send Ahmed out to sit at the gate where the businessmen sat and give out fliers for the business. Andy the photographer arrived at the shop and told her his good news.

"My connection with the ad agency has been noticed so I have been asked to do a celebrity shoot, and I accepted."

"That's down to your amazing pictures more like…" Suzie said, "…and well deserved."

"Wanna come?"

"Do I ever!" Suzie cried.

"You don't even know who the celebrities are yet."

"Don't care! It will be fun."

"Okay then. None of the celebs are famous really… all 'B listers'… But I'll get the tickets sorted."

Ahmed returned with excited tales of the new business leads he had managed to secure. This, together with some intel from Cactus Girl, meant that they would exceed the sales target for this month. Suzie was overjoyed.

There was more good news later that day when she received a text from Christine in the UK. Christine had received a promotion to 'Section Leader'. Suzie WhatsApped her a virtual hug with a glass of champagne emoji and received a pig dancing the Highland Fling in return.

*

The next morning she thanked Cactus Girl and told her that her information had caused Suzie to do well. The girl seemed pleased.

"He is gone," she said, pointing to the space where the carpet man's stall usually stood.

"Gone?" Suzie repeated.

"Yes. Always this time each year. But he will be back." She explained about the annual Berber excursion he took each year. Suzie had heard that as part of the collective, Carpet Man would be a crucial part of the massive ad campaign that was about to start, but he was now missing. What was going on?

Chapter 15

Fame and Fortune

The ad campaign was a huge success, and Eric told her that Carpet Man had been a large part of that success before he left. In fact, it had gone so well that Eric had uncharacteristically given Suzie money to do up the shop. She hired builders and decorators, and immediately set them to work. With a lick of paint, some marble countertops, and new styling it was looking almost as swanky as HQ. Instead of just a counter there was now a proper reception area with comfortable seats for customers and a dedicated area for the print shop. One of the staffrooms at the back was converted to a boardroom, and a small room for private business transactions. The latter was furnished tastefully with mint tea 'on tap' for business customers. This was proving very popular with the locals.

*

Suzie had seen Farid Burhan on TV several times as she never missed an episode of *So You Think You Can Do Business*. Farid's name apparently meant 'incomparable knowledgeable one' in Arabic, which was very fitting for someone in his position.

Suzie pinched herself. She could not believe she was actually sitting on the black leather sofa strewn with tapestries outside his office with all the other candidates. She had a real rollercoaster of emotions going on. Excitement bubbled up mixed with nerves and apprehension. Even a bit of UK homesickness raised its ugly head. This had first appeared after the big UK meeting last month but thankfully this was now gradually ebbing away again. Breathing deeply, she steadied her nerves and looked over towards Isabel, who had no such concerns. The boardroom was where she performed best. Suzie could see that Isabel was ready to be 'up and at 'em'.

Farid's PA uttered the celebrated line, "Farid is ready now," and the group filed into his illustrious office. She had seen this office many times before on TV but it was a little more imposing in the flesh somehow.

Farid's 'right hand men' were immaculately dressed and already seated at a large table when they all walked in. They just stared at the candidates po-faced, which silenced the excited banter immediately.

Farid walked into the room. *"Bonjour, candidates."* His French was impeccable and they all hung on his every word of welcome, such was the power of his simple words that Suzie had totally forgotten that the TV cameras were filming this. They received the customary warning that 'charlatans would be ousted' and 'talent would therefore surface' and were then driven to the candidate hotel where they were expected to stay until the first task the next day. It was to be a sales pitch.

*

Next morning, Suzie was awoken by an early morning phone call so she quickly scampered into action. She had anticipated this and had laid out her clothes the night before. She ate the breakfast bar she had laid on top and found that she had beaten the rush to the bathroom. Looking in the mirror, she applied more than her usual amount of lippy and decided she would show the world what she was made of. She would be 'saleswoman of the year' in this first task or die trying.

Isabel emerged from the bathroom opposite, still in her white dressing gown and slippers. "Get a move on, Isabel! The cars will be here in a few minutes!" Suzie said.

"Alright, alright! Keep your hair on!"

Ten minutes later the cars pulled up and Isabel made it just in time, without full make-up. They grabbed their bags and joined the other eager beavers who were descending into the waiting taxis. En route the air was electric; the taxi was alive with tall tales of extraordinary selling powers and business prowess. The candidates were already competing for 'airtime' to get their views across in the hope they would influence the others. Within twenty minutes they alighted at the main medina souk and Suzie realised that Isabel was now standing there with her full make-up on. How could it look that perfect when she must have done it en route?

The place they entered was huge and Suzie realised

she had not seen this part of the souk before. A wonderful mixture of cuisines greeted her nostrils. They had been put into three teams, told to find a team name, choose a team leader, make two fast-food snacks, and sell them. Whoever sold most items by the end of the day would win the challenge.

Suzie knew she would find it hard but it was actually harder than she expected. However, she had come on this to learn so she decided to push herself as much as she could. She had been great at giving suggestions about what would be popular to eat but having made no sales at all for the first hour she decided to watch a guy who seemed to be charming the birds off the trees. He had a wonderfully natural way of coaxing people into buying. They were actually thanking him too. She could tell from her carpet man training that this was due to the guy respecting them, in true Berber fashion. She decided to do the same. Twenty minutes later, Suzie had made her first sale and by the end of the day she wasn't exactly 'saleswoman of the year', but her sales effort was not too shabby. Pleased with the result, she felt certain she would be out of the firing line, literally, but she was not sure how the other teams had got on. She had originally intended to make a note of how they were doing, but as she had been constantly striving to prove her own worth, she had forgotten. She had been barely aware of Farid's observer or the TV cameras either, which was probably a good thing.

Isabel, who had volunteered immediately for the team leader role one of the other teams, was nowhere to be seen immediately after the task. Suzie then spotted her 10 minutes later under some trees doing a piece to camera. Typical!

At 6pm, they all sat waiting once more outside Farid's boardroom, this time a little quieter. Once inside, Farid's observers went over the sales figures.

"For Team Aspire – *Qus* – sales were a total of 9,607.45 dirham, around £753 with Isabel coming top for sales made." No surprise there. She had often said she could sell ice to Innuits and Suzie believed her. "For Team Excalibur – *Breeh* – sales were a total of 9,556.42 dirham, £749 with Mark coming top for sales. For Team Nomad – Badawiin – sales were a total of 6,443.24 dirham, £505 with Jean-Paul coming top for sales. This means that Team Aspire has therefore won the first task." There were a few protests from Mark's team as their pride has been dented, but Farid was not listening. Verbal fingers were being pointed at a nice quiet guy with glasses and frizzy hair despite the fact that he had had one of the best sales figures in the losing team. As Suzie sat listening, she realised she had come second highest in her team. Happy days!

Farid's next remark was directed at Jean-Paul. "Who are you bringing back into the boardroom?" Jean Paul motioned to the guy with frizzy hair and glasses, and a guy named Mohammed. "The rest of you go back to the house. You three, wait outside for a few minutes. Me and my observers will discuss how you did. Jean-Paul, consider carefully and decide who failed this task." Suzie breathed a sigh of relief. The winning team and Suzie's team streamed out the office and congratulated Isabel and Mark. The first ordeal was over and they had survived. To

Isabel's disgust there was no winning team treat, just the satisfaction of a job well done.

Back at the candidate hotel, it became clear that the frizzy-haired guy with glasses was off the programme when he did not return. Poor guy.

They now had a couple of days before the next task and the candidate hotel was way more fun than people watching the show realised. The camera men only appeared at early mornings and after firings, so the candidates found entertaining ways of letting their hair down in between. One guy had a drinking game that was positively hilarious. There was another game where you had to stack shots of beer on your forehead. "Come on!" another candidate shouted. "I've got a great one. I need a helper. Isabel, you can be my helper. We stay in here and the rest of you come in one by one, and then just copy what we do." They all filed out obediently. The first person went in and closed the door behind them. Shrieks erupted from the room behind the closed door followed by raucous laughter. The second person went in – again shrieks were heard. What were they doing? It sounded hilarious. As each person went in and the same thing happened so the anticipation got higher and higher. It was now Suzie's turn. She turned the doorknob and went in. As the door closed behind her, the person that had just gone in before her slapped her hard around the face. The others in the room shrieked with laughter.

"What the hell is going on?" Suzie gasped.

"Each person that comes through the door has to slap the next person. We've all done it."

"Oh… well… I am the last one," Suzie said. The room

collapsed in laughter and they all flopped down onto the many seats. It wasn't until two hours later that Suzie realised that Ellie had been nowhere to be seen since the very start of the slap game. She decided to go looking for her. Each bedroom was empty, no Ellie. Where could she be? She looked outside, nobody there either. She wasn't sure what made her do this but she began to look in all the wardrobes. In the last and biggest one she found Ellie crouching there in the dark.

"Suzie! Is the game finished? Don't make me go in there... please!"

"What are you doing in here?" Suzie asked.

"I heard the shrieks and didn't know what was going on. I thought I was safest in here..." Ellie said nervously. "Is it over?" she asked again.

"It finished two hours ago!" Suzie said. "You can come out now."

Ellie breathed a sigh of relief and stepped out of the wardrobe.

"Look who I found!" Suzie said when they entered the main room together. A cheer went up.

"Where've you been, Ellie? We thought Farid had fired you!" they shouted. Ellie was vague about her whereabouts and Suzie was not about to tell them. What kind of person hides in a wardrobe for two hours?

*

At 7am the next morning the candidates were driven to her ad agency headquarters, yes! Her very own workplace! Farid explained that some of the most appealing adverts came

111

from this place, and he wanted all three teams to design an advert to sell cactus-fruit products. This was a brand-new trend that the health conscious were taking seriously.

Suzie surprised herself and put herself forward to be team leader for this one, as it was a no-brainer. She started by telling everyone to look up the properties of cactus fruit on their mobile phones. It transpired that the fruit lowers blood pressure and cholesterol, protects against sunburn and skin ageing, and prevents dehydration. They were even anti-inflammatory, low fat and low calorie, what was not to like? Suzie became excited and asked people which roles they preferred according to their skills. Within twenty minutes they had a plan, roles were allocated, and the advert was underway.

Later that day in the boardroom, all three adverts were shown. Team Aspire had made a video about people wanting a drink in the desert. They had put beads of water on the fruit to suggest they were straight from the fridge (preposterous in the heat of the desert), but it got the message across that these fruits hydrate. Team Nomad had done a totally bad-taste one about people 'burning to a crisp' until they found cactus fruit. Time for her team's offering. As the images flickered across the screen, she found a sense of pride rising at the result.

Suzie had decided to go with the suggestion to present the fruit with a song: 'What you gonna do if you're in a state? Cactus fruit! What you gonna do if you want to lose weight? Cactus fruit! What you gonna do when you look like a prune? Cactus fruit! What you gonna do if you need suncream soon? Cactus fruit!' and so on. This allowed all of the cactus-fruit properties to be seen in an entertaining way. Slightly cheesy but good fun to watch. The two other teams roared with laughter when they saw her team's advert and it was the only one to have a soundtrack. Farid announced his decision. Suzie's team had won! However, Team Nomad (*Badawiin*) was in the firing line again. Back at the hotel it was clear that Badawiin's team leader was off the programme when they did not return.

*

After a pleasant and relaxed weekend they were called in for the third task. For this one they had to set up a spice stall at the souk but source a list of vague items to sell. Team Aspire bombed tragically due to lack of local knowledge and Isabel was brought into the boardroom. The customary accusations between candidates flew around but Isabel somehow managed to 'schmooze' her way out of trouble.

*

Task four two days later was about setting up business with the Bedouins in the Agafay desert. This task was absolutely made for Suzie so she put herself forward again as team leader. This time, however, the vote went to Mohammed to be team leader, who had been moved from another team by Farid. Jeeps came to collect them bright and early and then all of them were given a camel and a compass. They had to make their way in the desert and do business with some Bedouins Farid had already spoken to. They should arrive and present their business ideas and get home before dark. This seemed simple enough but Suzie knew this would be strenuous due to the midday heat and shifting sands. They had been told that Farid's observers were experienced in the desert and could step in if teams were lost, but this would incur a time penalty.

Ten minutes into the task they came across some cactus fruit. In true 'Carpet Man fashion' Suzie suggested they pick them. "No!" Mohammed had said. Suzie ignored this command and started picking them. "We're not waiting for you," Mohammed shouted. Fine, she would catch up. It would only take a few seconds and may be a lifesaver later on. The team carried on and left her behind. Within five minutes Suzie had caught up and by midday they had not found the Bedouins yet. It was getting seriously hot. Suzie pulled out her water bottle. It was at this point that she realised none of the others had brought a water bottle so she shared out the cactus fruit. She thought she recognised this place. Carpet Man's 'oasis' was five minutes away, where they could rest from the heat, plan their next move, and get water supplies. However, Mohammed shouted her down as it was 'too far out of the way' and 'who is she to know, anyway?'. Two hours later, the team were flagging in the heat. And with no Bedouins or the meeting place in sight, Farid's observer stepped in to rescue the situation. The team arrived back at the starting point after dark. Three team members had heat exhaustion, and they had absolutely no business to show for their efforts. Man, it would be bad in the boardroom tomorrow. Mohammed would definitely be in the firing line.

"So," Farid said. "What happened to Team Excalibur?"

The observer told Farid how Mohammed had been decisive, but it had not led to any business. He also said that he had had to step in to get them back. "Not good. This means you have the time penalty too. Who are you bringing back, Mohammed?"

Mohammed thought for a moment. "There is only one person really at fault here. Suzie."

"What?" Suzie was amazed. "I was giving you both time and life-saving suggestions. At one point you could have got our team killed from heatstroke, you had no water, no realistic plan to meet the Bedouins … I mean, what actually was the business plan?" This felt like a slap in the face and Suzie was unusually blunt.

"Enough!" Farid said. "You two stay here. The rest of you go back to the hotel. Mohammed, tell me why you are bringing Suzie back in." Mohammed had an old-fashioned view of women and explained about how 'disruptive' and 'disrespectful' Suzie had been, and how she had even 'disobeyed a command' right at the start to pick cactus fruit. She should not have been so blunt just now but he was making her out to be some sort of 'loose cannon'. She was not going to stand for that but could see how this would not go down well with Farid, and she was right. Amid her protestations the dreaded words were uttered and she found herself in a car with her bags backed, heading back to her own flat.

*

The following week she was dying to hear how Isabel was getting on. This show was aired a week after the footage had been shot so she didn't have to wait long. In fact, Isabel didn't last much longer than her, only one task longer and had appeared back at work three days thereafter. Isabel had put herself forward for team leader again for a 'pop-up shop' task. She had delegated all jobs out to her team and done nothing herself. The team had actually seen through her crafty ways and rounded on her for being lazy. This was not the blaze of glory she would want to go out on, that's for sure.

Work colleagues congratulated both Suzie and Isabel, and Isabel had of course said that she had been managing the team well on the last task but the team were jealous of her. *Keep telling yourself that*, Suzie thought. Their work colleagues also seemed to think that Suzie was wrongly dismissed and had to leave much too soon. Suzie caught sight of Isabel, who was silent. Isabel did not even look at her. Even Suzie's mum had sent a gift to her with the word 'daughter' written on it. This may not sound a lot but Mum had never been that 'effusive' before. So why now?

Chapter 16

The 'Cactus Girl'

The TV experience had taught Suzie one thing – that when you can't control the results, don't worry about them. It was weird how letting go of total control had meant that she felt more in control than she had ever been. A real revelation.

Suzie sat on her balcony, pouring herself a mug of steaming coffee from the cafetière. She watched as the cactus girl set out her stall. The girl waved at her, and so Suzie decided to go and talk to her. Suzie knew the girl still had no English so she spoke to the girl in French.

"Hello, *ma chérie*, how are you?"

"*D'accord*," came the reply.

"Do you like selling cactus fruit?"

The girl explained in French about how she had no choice but to sell them as she was the older sister.

"Carpet Man said your parents are not here, *je suis désolé*."

"I have no Mum or Dad. Just my sister. We sell these to pay for food."

Suzie realised there were no social services here. Crikey. The poor girl. This was all she could do. "But how do you survive?"

The girl told Suzie about how she followed Carpet Man wherever he went, and also the tourists to get the most business. "We get enough to buy food," she said. This explained why she was not always outside the flat. She was not, in fact, the naive 'lost girl' Suzie had supposed, but a girl who was very shrewd in her observations with a business sense beyond her years.

"*Chérie*, would you like a job at my shop when you get older?"

The girl looked thoughtful as she arranged the fruit on the tray. "*Peut-être. Merci.*"

*

The next day a sandstorm blew in from the east. It proved to be like nothing Suzie had ever seen or heard before.

"What's that?" Suzie cried. A sound like a large metal skip being dragged along the cobbled streets below the flat filled the air. As she got up to investigate she realised that it was the sound of the approaching sandstorm! She could see a blanket of brown beyond her flat balcony where there should have been a view. She quickly closed all the windows, doors, and window shutters just in time before it made its way into the flat. Phew!

She had never imagined that a sandstorm could be so 'noisy'. In the city they were protected from the worst of it, but all employees had nevertheless been told to stay at home that day until the storm had passed, and

Suzie understood why now. It would have been utterly impossible to be out in that.

The storm raged all morning and just when it had settled down it was followed by a swarm of locust, each at least nine centimetres long. They were just like giant grasshoppers on steroids! Locals were picking them off their wares for sale and throwing them to one side, as if swotting commonplace flies away. Again, Suzie had never seen anything like this before. She understood for the first time how a swarm of these things could decimate a field of crops in minutes.

Of course, Cactus Girl was nowhere to be seen during all of this, thank God, but she was also missing on the days that followed. For that matter, Carpet Man was not there either and Suzie wondered if he had taken her to do business elsewhere.

*

Once back at work, to Suzie's frustration there was still the accusatory undercurrent of 'missing accounts' and a general sense of unease going on at HQ. Her TV experience had taught her that as this was not something she could control she would try to ignore it as best she could. So she ignored the staring eyes, the questioning looks and defensive behaviour and imagined swotting these away just like the locals had done earlier with the locust. Six months ago this would have eaten away at her – a biting animal gnawing away at her sanity. But not now. She was stronger in all respects.

"Best get to it," she said as she busied herself with the

next task. Both UK and Moroccan ad agency departments were doing a combined promotion of Morocco as a desirable holiday destination. She arranged some excellent images Andy had taken for her for the promo flier and decided on the typeset style. Many of the photos would look great in the brochure too.

Carpet Man had been crucial to setting up the collaboration with the local co-operative but did not want to be acknowledged for it. 'I am only a collaborator,' he had said. In fact, he had remained distant since Suzie had appeared on Farid's programme, but his mentoring had taught her how to suss out the 'local vibe'. This resulted in her doing well on the tasks on the TV show tasks and she wanted to thank Carpet Man. Was he mad at her for not acknowledging him on TV? No, that can't be it. Not really his style. So, what then? Suzie didn't know and his semi-flirting moment had confused her.

It is true that Suzie liked the carpet man, she liked him a lot in fact. But that did not make it love. If anything, it was more a kind of sincere admiration for the kind of life he had chosen and the genuine person that he was. It was a kind of heartfelt gratitude and respect that a daughter feels for a father when offering advice out of his extensive life experience in order to prevent some future catastrophe.

There was a rumour going around in the office at one point that Carpet Man was her 'sugar daddy' but where on earth that had come from was anyone's guess. Suzie suspected it was Isabel as it was only really her that knew about her excursions out to test the local cuisine. Only the other day, a new guy in marketing had told her that a man who pretends to be rich in order to attract a young woman is not a 'sugar daddy'. Suzie had thought that he was about to stand up for her but then he followed it up with a quip about the carpet man being 'an artificial sweetener' instead. There were other jokes circulating about the 'number of rugs she must have back at the flat', and others about how Carpet Man could 'pull the rug from under her feet' or 'pull the wool over her eyes'. None of them were funny.

This stirred up a curious mixture of emotions. Protectiveness towards Carpet Man, as he did not warrant any of this and neither did she for that matter, and irritation concerning the juvenile jibes. It was difficult to believe that she had only met Carpet Man six months ago because of the impact he had already had on her. It was as if she had known him all her life. He was quietly charismatic and matter of fact by nature. Suzie could see that the wandering Berber life had had a great effect on him and his way of thinking. This would have caused many people to have been 'remote' and unable to converse easily with city-dwellers, but up until now the reverse had been true. He had a hypnotic wisdom when he spoke which engendered a kind of reverent trust in those that listened.

Suzie thought back to the time she had first seen him setting out his carpets outside the flat window. She remembered that he had been nothing like some of the other carpet-stall salesmen despite the fact he owned a carpet showroom (which she knew about from her day in the Agafay desert). Other salesmen were pushy. She didn't want the carpets when she passed their stalls, however much of a bargain they were, but many would not listen.

To one of them, who had been particularly pushy on one occasion, Suzie offered to give him her sunglasses by way of distraction – and it worked. The guy was delighted. He immediately forgot that he was trying to sell her his carpet and gave Suzie a gift as compensation for her kindness.

No. Admiring reverence did not make it love.

Late that afternoon, after work, Suzie spotted Cactus Girl gathering up her cactus fruit with a girl around seven or eight years of age. Dust left from the sandstorm that had passed through was being kicked up from the ground when motorbikes passed, and the slight breeze was swirling the dust around like a chiffon scarf. A little old woman across the square was trying to brush up some of the sand to one side with a stick-like brush.

Here was Cactus Girl caring for her sister and teaching her a trade. Many people would have judged this book by the cover and completely dismissed both of them, but not Carpet Man. And now not Suzie either. She noted that there was no longer a look of desperation about Cactus Girl. Yes, she definitely seemed to ooze contentment these days, and Suzie began to understand why.

Chapter 17

Trouble at Mill

The phone rang. Suzie was sitting up at her desk in the shop going over the weekly accounts. "Have you heard the news, Suzie?" It was Tony.

"What?"

"You might want to lie low today, they are gunning for you over here."

"What on earth for?"

"Dunno, but there is major shit going down here. Just thought I better warn you."

Silently, she put the phone down. She racked her brains. There was nothing she could think of that could possibly explain this. The phone rang again, this time it was Eric.

"Please bring your notebook and weekly accounts with you when you come over to the HQ meeting in a few minutes, we have important matters to discuss." His tone was clipped. What was going on? Suzie hurriedly gathered her things and went over to Eric's office at HQ.

"Take a seat," Eric said. He then motioned to a man sitting to the right of him, dressed in a dark suit. "This is an observer, just ignore him. Okay. Let's get straight down to business. How much do you know about the Paterson account?"

"Not much. I know it is a UK one and that it is linked to one here in Morocco and that's about it." Was this some kind of test?

"And what about our biggest current ad campaign, how much do you know about that?"

"I obviously know quite a bit as I designed it. I could describe what most other people did on that score too. You know all this." She paused. "I think it should be a huge success."

"It will be nothing of the sort!" Eric retorted. "A rival company has got wind of it just as it was about to be launched. They have stolen it, are now suing us, and are now accusing *us* of stealing it from them."

"What! Oh, man…" Suzie's mouth went dry.

"Exactly. So you had better tell us everything you know, right now. Where did you get the idea for the original ad campaign from?"

"It came to me when I was in the lift one day." Suzie noticed that Eric had her campaign proposal in his hand. "If you look on page three of the document you are holding you will see it described there in great detail." Eric looked, and the suited observer made notes. "Isabel said that you stole it from her, what do you have to say to that?"

"Did she tell you where she supposedly got the idea from? I am guessing not because I can assure you that I have never had to steal anything in my whole life."

"Isabel said that you had made a habit of nicking her ideas and this time it really shocked her."

"I told you. I have never and would never resort to that kind of behaviour. If you look on page fifteen you will see how I developed the idea. It is all there in your document."

"You seem to know the details of this document very well. Have you been memorising it?"

"No need to memorise it – I wrote it!" Suzie's heart thumped. Deep shit indeed. The suited man wrote more notes. It was clear that Isabel had taken credit for her report, so what else had she been saying?

"I am going to be blunt," Eric snarled. "Did you leak details from our biggest-ever ad campaign to the rival agency?"

"Which agency? What are you talking about? No! Definitely not! How could you even think it was me?" The neighbouring offices could tell something was going on as raised voices could be heard for the next half hour coming from Eric's office.

When they were finished with her, Suzie stormed out. "Oh, man, she stitched me up like a kipper!" This uncharacteristic outburst was met by a mixture of bemused and glaring faces as she passed. There was even someone openly laughing at Suzie.

"Kipper?" they said. "Where the hell did you get that saying from? Eighteenth-century England?" Their whole office laughed. Suzie ignored this and kept walking. She was heartily sick of Isabel's manipulative games that nobody else seemed to notice, and now she had thrown her under the bus or framed her. She knew nothing of how it had all gone so tragically wrong. Eric had the wrong end of the stick as usual. Did he believe Suzie? He had actually threatened disciplinary action if she didn't own up. She struggled to take it all in but had restated that she had nothing to own up to. Had someone *really* sold the ad agency down the river? She didn't know, the only thing she *did* know was that Eric was very, very angry. That cow, Isabel, had done it again. But this time she had gone too far. This time, there would be a major penalty for someone to pay.

Suzie knew Isabel would be doing her usual 'yes, sir, no, sir, is there anything I can do to help, sir?' routine when she had been summoned into Eric's office. Suzie now understood perfectly that Isabel could sell her own grandmother down the river if it meant acquiring a Gucci handbag in her place. Someone Suzie used to know had a saying: 'If they fell face first into pig shit they would still come back up smelling of roses'. For the first time ever, Suzie knew what they meant. Suzie had always known deep down since coming to Morocco that Isabel was not all she claimed to be but had put that down to insecurities. But to sell out their prize campaign to a rival? Isabel's very own best friend's campaign? That was really low. She wondered if Isabel had attempted to warn Suzie about her treacherous plans in her own warped way, but when going over the events from the past week she realised quickly there was absolutely no evidence of this. It had been totally planned that Suzie should be the fall guy. How could she have been so stupid? Suzie had even taken Isabel's off-handed ways to be jealousy about Suzie's better results these days. She just had to do something but couldn't focus enough to do anything.

She sat at her desk typing any old rubbish like an

automaton to make it look like she was fine and working as normal. But she wasn't. She decided to take the post down to the post room to try and shake herself free from her state of disbelief. What the hell was she going to do? She pushed the visions in her mind away that clamoured to crowd her head. Visions of her sister standing with her arms folded across her chest saying, 'I told you so.' Visions of her boyfriend silently glaring at her. Visions of her mum shaking her head and saying over and over, 'Wrong choices, Suzanne, wrong choices.' As she walked slowly down the long corridor the weight of her heart was so heavy in her chest that it seemed to be pulling her physically downwards, like a heavy sack dragging along the ground. She so wanted this job to be a success. The culture, work, and the people were great. She loved the ethos of this place and for the first time in her life she could actually see herself settling down. Every time she thought like this the carpet man would enter her head for some reason. It was obviously because he seemed to be truly happy with his life, unlike most people.

Toby, the office clown, popped his head out when Suzie passed his office. She could see he was about to make some amusing comment at Suzie's expense. However, having seen the look of utter devastation on her face he thought better of it and remained silent for once. Seriously. How could she have been so stupid?

*

The next day she and Tony were sitting at the coffee machine.

"You know they pulled me in there too, don't you?" Tony said.

"No! But you are the most dependable person here!"

"Maybe so, but that didn't stop them accusing me. I felt like I was being framed."

"Oh," Suzie said. "You too? They did that to me."

"It must have been someone with the opportunity," Tony said in hushed tones. "You had a big part in the campaign but it was your baby and you were at the shop. You couldn't have witnesses back at the shop and be here at HQ at the same time, so I know it's definitely not you."

"Thanks... I think." Suzie breathed.

Tony continued. "It could have been Toby. He left the office early the day before the launch saying he had a dentist appointment."

"Do we know when it happened?" Suzie asked. "When was somebody supposed to have approached the other ad agency?"

"Nobody really knows. I guess it could have been Ahmed from the shop as he was over here helping the day before the launch. In fact, he had motive and opportunity. He has always wanted to 'play with the big boys' and was left alone in the boardroom finishing up the font inconsistencies when we all left."

"No! It's not Ahmed. He is really dependable too. He's a great guy. I can't believe it!"

"Face it, Suzie, it's definitely someone. And people are not always who they seem."

Ain't that the truth, she thought, but something kept Suzie from saying that she was almost sure she knew who had done it. As if reading her mind Tony continued.

"There's also Isabel. Now she couldn't have done it because I was with her the whole time." This was a revelation to Suzie. She had assumed that Isabel had slipped out at some point like she used to do when living at the flat. Isabel often did a disappearing act in her usual day to day life at work too, so this would be a first if she had really been there all the time. In fact, her being there the whole time was *definitely* suspicious. "That just leaves us with Toby really," he finished. As far as she knew, Toby didn't have a reason for framing her, or Tony for that matter.

"Tony, I hate to ask... did they threaten you with disciplinary action?"

"Yes, total bullshit if you ask me. I've been here three years without a spot on my record. I reckon they just wanted to frighten people into telling the truth." If that was the case, Suzie was pretty sure that Eric's threats would have had no effect on Isabel whatsoever.

All those that had been hauled into the office had been told that they had to remain working at HQ whilst they investigated, and that included Suzie.

*

Each day she and Tony would meet at the coffee machine to discuss their latest suspicions.

"I reckon if it wasn't Toby the culprit must have done it after work. If that's the case, we may all be under suspicion. Fortunately, I was at a ticketed music evening all night so they can't accuse me. Where were you, Suzie?"

"Oh, man. I had an evening in, washing my hair. That leaves me wide open as a target – with no alibi."

"Hmm, yes. And what about Toby? Do we know what he did?" Suzie shook her head. "Maybe that's the first thing we need to do. Find out where he was that night." Suzie agreed.

A great opportunity presented itself when she had to take some stills to Toby later that morning. "Ah, come to give me some sexy pictures," he drawled.

Creep. "No, but these should be exactly what you are looking for. So tiresome this 'leak' thing, isn't it?"

He looked up at her. "They got you in there too?"

Something in the way he said that told Suzie that he had been questioned too that day. She ignored his question and instead said, "I reckon they will be checking out all our alibis soon." Toby paled but said nothing. "I reckon you'll be okay though because you had a dentist appointment." Damn it. She wasn't supposed to know about that.

"Uh," Toby replied. He was non-committal. "Better get back to work."

"Yes, see you later, Toby."

*

Back at the coffee machine the next day Suzie reported her conversation with Toby. "Sounds like they questioned him too. By the way he acted I reckon he was not at the dentist that afternoon, but I am not convinced it was him."

"Well surely that proves it? Motive and opportunity? I reckon it was him. I'm going to track his every movement."

"If we have not actually spoken to the alleged dentist, we can't really know for sure, can we?"

"I'm going to do just that."

"How?" Suzie asked.

Tony touched his nose conspiratorially. "Leave it to me…"

*

The next time Suzie saw Tony he had news for her. "Spoke to Toby and said I was looking for a dentist. He put me onto his one. I booked an emergency appointment, talked about some fake pain I had with them, and name-dropped Toby and his recent appointment. Taking me to be a friend of his, the dentist recounted some of Toby's conversation so he was definitely there, just as he said. I thought we had drawn a blank until the dentist made a chance remark about Toby being 'under time pressure for meeting someone at the souk' and handed me something Toby had dropped on his way out. It was a handwritten note. The dentist asked me to give it to Toby as it seemed to be important."

"What did the note say?"

"It just said: 'Mohammed, Stall Fifteen, 4pm."

It was too much to resist and Suzie desperately wanted to find the culprit to eradicate the wild accusations she was getting, so she agreed to go to the souk the next day with Tony. As there were several souks in the city, they had to first locate the right one. This would not be easy. They found that there were two possible Stall Fifteens. The first was a beauty stall run by a young girl. She was definitely not named Mohammed. In the second souk Stall Fifteen turned out to be a herb stall with baskets of rosemary, wild oregano, and other herbs piled high. She and Tony had dressed in European clothing and pretended to be a couple here on holiday. A tall, burly man with a bushy black beard stood with his arms folded at the front of the stall. His eyes never left them even once as they perused his wares.

"Come on, let's go," Tony said. Once out of earshot he exclaimed, "Did you see that guy? Reckon he is Mohammed. Right shady if you ask me."

"He certainly looks dodgy, but how are we going to find out why Toby was there without asking him? How can we see if there is a link between this dodgy guy and the rival ad company?" Suzie said.

"Dunno. But I reckon it's definitely Toby…"

*

It never was explained who the suited guy was in Eric's office the day they had all been hauled into the office, nor why he was making notes. Judging by the events that happened next, wheels seemed to have been put into motion. Suzie was due to do a big presentation to a large gathering of local businessmen but was told by Eric she was 'no longer required' and that he would be doing it instead. Was this because he thought she was the culprit? Or because Suzie had dared to imply that his favourite protégé Isabel was less than perfect? She didn't know… but she was going to find out.

Chapter 18

The T&S Detective Agency

Tony arranged to meet Suzie at the café opposite her flat the next day as he said he had a new lead on the 'leak'. It was Sunday, and she found him sitting in a secluded corner. He had already ordered them some drinks so they got to work immediately.

"Toby's alibi checked out okay at the dentist but if the deed was done after work he is definitely in the frame because we don't know why he went to the dodgy stallholder or what he did afterwards, do we? With all that herb stuff on the stall… you don't think he's doing drugs?"

"No! That's ridiculous. That's how Moroccans make mint tea! How long have you been here, Tony? Anyway, Toby doesn't really look the 'type'. Are there any more suspects? I am guessing that is why you wanted to meet outside of work," Suzie said.

"There are. I did a bit of sniffing around. It could be that young casual worker they took on in accounts a few weeks ago."

"Who? Mo?"

"Yes. He says he was 'doing nothing' on the day in question and so has no alibi... and wait for it... neither has Eric."

Suzie breathed. "Eric is vague at the best of times, but I guess that doesn't necessarily make him the culprit."

"True, but I saw him with my own eyes fishing stuff out of the wastepaper bin the other day."

"What? You think he was trying to retrieve some sort of guilty document that may incriminate him?"

"Yes," Tony said. "Face it. He is clever enough to have done it. The 'powers that be' still don't know who did it or when. At least we have narrowed down the time frame."

"What about Amy? I can't put my finger on it, but she always looks a bit shifty."

"Perhaps we should do a bit more surveillance. I'll take Mo and you take Amy. Eric will be tricky so we will both have to keep our eyes on him."

Suzie still had not been allowed to return to her shop but she had no doubt that Andy would be doing a great job while she was at HQ. This at least meant she had the opportunity to keep a close eye on Amy. Suzie invented lots of plausible ways to interact with or follow Amy: 'Amy, could I bother you to look at this please?', 'Amy, Eric has sent me over with these documents', 'Amy, do you fancy a coffee?' Suzie noted that Amy, like Isabel, often disappeared for twenty minutes at a time during her normal working day. That had to put her under suspicion, right? On one occasion she followed her into the ladies but to her astonishment when she pushed the door open nobody was in there. The sliding glass door onto the balcony had been left ajar. The next balcony along was so close that anyone fairly agile could have climbed over into it. As Amy was nowhere to be seen and had not come out of the loo the only answer was that she must have climbed over the balcony. But why?

Then there was Eric. He had certainly put her under pressure on the day he interrogated her. Was that him trying to deflect his own blame? He was certainly the kind of person that would do that without worrying about it. As the photocopier was right outside his office and the glass wall between meant that she could watch his movements when standing there, she hoped nobody would ask why she suddenly had lots of photocopying to do. Most of the time there was nothing of note, but she noticed that at 10.30am every morning he made or received a call.

*

Today Eric had been called to her shop to go and sort out something, something she would have normally dealt with herself. It stung, but on the upside it meant that she had free reign to check his HQ phone while he was gone. It was one of those phones that had a memory on it so now all she had to do was check the recent calls and see which ones were made at 10.30am. As she scrolled down the list she found it. A call to Treece and Floggs ad agency, at exactly 10.30am yesterday. She looked at the day before. There it was again, 'Treece and Floggs, 10.30am'. "Gotcha!" she cried.

At the coffee machine at break Tony told her how Mo from accounts had a dark secret. "I wasn't sure why but he was missing regularly for periods at a time during work hours so I decided to have it out with him. I collared him and accused him straight out but he said he suspected Eric. He said Eric was 'not to be trusted' because Mo had been checking all monies in and out, had noticed discrepancies, but been too frightened to say anything. You see, Eric has to check that all the balances tally and Mo said that they often didn't, but Eric let them go through unbalanced."

"Hmm. That does place him under suspicion," Suzie agreed. She told him about Amy's disappearing act and her 'sudden need' to photocopy. "Get this, Tony, Eric also makes a call to Treece and Floggs at 10.30am each day."

"Whoa! We've got him! It's him then! But what the heck do we do about it?"

"Hold on a minute, it could be legit. We need to check each of these leads out first."

The hushed tones were suddenly pierced with a shrill cry. "Check *what* out, may I ask?"

"Amy!" Tony cried. Neither of them had heard her come in. How long had she been there?

"Come on, what are you two up to? Check what out?" Amy asked. "Hope it's not me."

Suzie hesitated. "Admit it, Amy, you often disappear for up to twenty minutes every day and never say where you are going."

"You're crazy!" Amy replied. "The paranoia in this place has got to you too. It's been dreadful since the leak."

"Come on, Amy, humour me and prove your innocence. Where do you disappear to each day?"

"I'm not telling you."

"Come on, or I will tell Eric this minute. Where do you go?"

"I have irritable bowel syndrome, you freak! Happy now, are you? I keep it a secret because who wants a dynamic creative who can't deal with the tension of the job? Or this stupid atmosphere? You tell anyone and I will make it sound like discrimination!" Suzie thought this was not the best time to mention Amy's 'balcony disappearing act'. It would be difficult giving a plausible explanation as to why she had followed her into the loo, and then accused her of the leak. Bad move. Not well thought out on her part. Better leave it for now.

"Oh," said Tony, a little pink in the face. "Sorry, Amy." Amy turned and walked away without acknowledging his apology. "Definitely Eric then," Tony said softly to Suzie under his breath.

"But I thought we had narrowed down the time frame for the act as being after work?" Suzie said. "Not 10.30am."

"True. But either way, it is pretty dodgy that Eric phones a rival ad agency every day. We need to get to the bottom of that one."

Later that day, further news reached Suzie and Tony on the grapevine. Eric had been in with Mr Phipps (the ad agency's 'big boss') for the whole evening on the evening in question when the 'leak' had happened. They had both been interrogating employees one by one and trying to work out who was to blame.

"That means Eric could not have done it after work and is probably not him but we still need to follow up why he has been calling Treece and Floggs every day," Tony said.

"Agreed," Suzie said.

"I know. I will follow him. I have a week's holiday and he won't suspect a thing. If he was the culprit he may still be hastily covering his tracks so I might catch him in the act." Tony was resolute.

"This is like the Tony and Suzie Detective Agency," said Suzie excitedly. "T&S Detective Agency at your service!"

*

A week later Tony was back at work after his annual leave and had fresh news. He explained how he had followed Eric and for three days solid but there was nothing to report. On the fourth day Eric went to Treece and Floggs' ultra-modern building, built mainly of glass with state-of-the-art shutters. "As I stood outside I saw him reappear on the second floor only to be greeted by someone I know."

"Who? Tell me!"

"I couldn't remember her name but I know she sometimes used to do some freelance journalism for us. She did some work connected with one of the campaigns I did a couple of years ago. Eric went to greet her with a kiss but she turned away."

"So… Eric knows this woman?"

"Yes, looks like he more than *knows* her, if you know what I mean. I got the impression she was not happy to see him."

"Did you see anything else?"

"No, but I checked this morning what that ad campaign was that she worked on with us. Her name is Jane Reynolds. I also checked on Treece and Floggs website to double check whether Jane works there, and bingo! She does. So, what do we do now? Go straight to Mr Phipps?"

"No. I'm inclined to wait for a bit. I agree that it looks ultra-dodgy but suppose there is some plausible explanation for it?"

"Come off it! Eric has been caught red-handed not only phoning a rival company but meeting with them in broad daylight? That's guilty as hell in my books. If he is covering his tracks all evidence might disappear soon and he will never be caught. We have to act fast."

Tony was right, of course, but first they had delve into Jane's part in all this. What did she know? Was it her that leaked their campaign to the press?

It was tricky. Tony and Suzie could not exactly ask Jane straight out if she knew about the leak. If she didn't know her journalist side would take over and she would have a scoop handed to her on a plate. What's more, that would certainly result in the two of them getting fired as the whole office had been told by their legal team not to discuss the situation with anyone. On the other hand, if she was involved they had to find out somehow if they were to prove their innocence.

They decided that they would pose as an SME company who wanted a small ad campaign to help sales. They said that because they were busy they could only come after 5pm, and Jane had agreed to make an appointment with them. When she asked why they had chosen her, they told her that they had seen her on the company website which, strictly speaking, was true.

*

Later that week they attended the meeting with Jane. She was petite and looked very professional in a Jaeger two piece. "How can I help?" Jane said. Suzie noted that she had the same phone type as Eric. Maybe all of these places had the same phones? They made up a plausible-sounding idea for sales and Jane assured them that Treece and Floggs would be able to deliver that at the cost they desired. They then asked a deliberately tricky question so that Jane had to 'go and check'.

"Quick!" shot Tony. "Check her phone! I'll keep her busy!" Suzie dashed over to the phone and scrolled through her list of 'recents'. In the 'received calls' list there it was! Eric's number. Just like they knew it would be. "Quick! She's coming back!" Suzie sat back in the chair just as Jane opened the door.

"You will need to make another appointment with me to go over those costs, as there could be some add-ins and we would need to discuss that further," Jane said.

"We could come at 10.30am tomorrow," Tony said.

Jane looked doubtful. "No, not 10.30am. I have another client booked then."

"Or 10.30am the next day?" Tony continued. Suzie kept quiet as she knew what he was doing.

"No. Apologies. I will get in touch with you to confirm when we can make the next appointment, goodbye." Jane shook their hands.

After leaving the building they stopped in the nearest narrow alleyway and went over what they knew. "So, we know for definite that Eric is phoning Jane and both their phones prove it. This also proves they know each other. Jane has the means to 'spill the beans' through her journalism sideline, and there is evidence that Eric could have done it with her help. But all this doesn't tell us *why* though..."

*

Over the next few weeks Tony and Suzie followed all possible leads but they never found a motive for Eric. It was all very frustrating. All leads seemed to have come to an end. So much for the T&S Detective Agency! The 'powers that be' seemed to have reached the same conclusion as little by little the heavy atmosphere seemed to dissipate at HQ. Nobody was told anything further, and apart from the odd titbit on the grapevine, Suzie heard nothing either. Maybe it had all blown over? Maybe they had found the culprit, sorted it, and now it was business as usual? All things seemed to point to this as she had been told she could return to working at her shop in the next few weeks. Maybe it hadn't been Eric after all, and not Isabel either, but she knew better than to ask them straight out.

At that moment Isabel stuck her head through the door. "Hear you are going back to your shop soon."

Suzie was guarded. "Yes. Can't say I am not sorry."

"Yeah, the atmosphere around here has been hell lately. They even thought *I'd* done it."

Suzie did not admit that she too had thought Isabel had been the perpetrator for a while. If she was honest, she still did. "Yeah, I will be glad to get back to normal."

Tony, sitting at the desk next to her, agreed.

141

Eric thundered into the room. "You two, my office, *now*!" he shouted without breaking his step.

"What the hell's going on now?" Tony asked. Suzie's face had a look of uncomprehending disbelief. They followed Eric into his office. He did not utter pleasantries to come in and sit down.

"I have just been informed that you two went to Treece and Floggs. Explain yourselves," he snarled.

Oh, man, busted. Tony and Suzie exchanged worried looks. How could they say they were following him as a lead as they thought he was the cause of the leak? Tony was first to talk after a short silence. "It's difficult."

"Try."

"We can't tell you."

"Need I tell you about the consequences that may happen if you don't co-operate? I might even enjoy them." Eric smirked.

"We really can't tell you," Tony said again. "But we were trying to find the cause of the leak." Sweat began to break out on his top lip. Suzie could see it glistening in the sunlight beaming from the window.

"And why go there? I saw the guilty looks you exchanged when you came in here. Trying to find the leak – really?"

"It wasn't guilt," Tony said defensively.

"What was it then? Anything you need to tell me?" Tony and Suzie looked at each other again. Silence. "Well then. Let me tell you what I know. I know you went to visit Jane Reynolds to set up a rival company, she costed an ad campaign and told me you aim to start fairly soon. Doing this and choosing Jane, who by the way is also a journalist, looks pretty damning on you two don't you think?"

142

"How do you know about this, may I ask? How do you even know if this rumour that we were there is true?" Tony said.

"Oh, you were there alright, Jane told me."

"And how did she come to tell you?" Tony continued. He must have some kind of death wish or something. Suzie kept wanting Tony to shut up but found to her frustration nothing came out. To her surprise it was Eric's turn to look flustered.

"I am not telling you, that is none of your business," he growled.

"Then you will understand why we cannot tell you," Tony finished. Checkmate. He had neatly given Eric a 'touché' moment. A veiled threat. If Eric was determined to put them in the frame, Eric now knew that they would put him in the frame too. It would all come out about the phone calls and visits he made to Treece and Floggs.

"Get out!" Eric roared.

Suzie and Tony emerged to find the whole of the main office next door staring at them. The office had obviously heard parts of the conversation, put two and two together and made seven. Each person looked down and suddenly busied themselves as they walked past. Suzie had to admit, she could see how it would look bad if you didn't know why she and Tony had been at Treece and Floggs that day. What a complete mess! But what to do about it?

Chapter 19

Facing the Music

Christmas was rapidly approaching and over the next few days, Suzie and Tony laid low and didn't even meet together for coffee at work. They kept their conversations outside of work time and wondered if even this may have made them seem suspicious. Suzie had started second guessing herself and it was exhausting. Today, she met Tony at a café near his flat.

"I keep heading towards two different ways of handling this," Suzie started. "Completely ignore it or go straight to Mr Phipps. I really don't know which to do."

"I think we need to blow it wide open and go straight to the top," Tony replied.

"What? Even if it means losing our jobs?" Suzie cried.

"You saw how people are avoiding us now. Toby even put salt in my coffee the other day when I wasn't looking."

"Yes I know what you mean. I opened my drawer this morning to find a piece of paper saying 'loser'. What kind of person does that when it's not even been proved if we did anything wrong?"

"Are we agreed then? One way or another we have to act?" Tony asked.

"Yes. It looks so bad for us now. I guess we don't have much to lose anymore. It stinks working in a place where paranoia reigns, accusations fly, and no one knows what is going on. It's not what I came here for." As Suzie said this she saw her sister's smirking face and her mother's 'I told you so' look in her mind's eye. She didn't want to face it but there was really no alternative now. This was no longer the 'fun job she thrived in'. Although she had been allowed back to the shop for small periods of time, there was no word of when she may be able to return properly. No word of when she may next get some light relief there.

The two of them bent their heads and drafted an e-mail to Mr Phipps, the big boss, explaining that ordinarily they would not dream of doing this but this was an extraordinary time. They explained how their trip to Treece and Floggs was motivated out of loyalty to the firm to follow leads and find the culprit, and not the act of treachery that Eric clearly thought it was. They were not sure how much Mr Phipps knew about the leak situation as he was never around, but they had nothing to lose now. Either way, Eric would be impossible, so nothing new there. On the day the ad agency broke up for Christmas they sent the e-mail. No looking back now.

Suzie did not much feel like celebrating Christmas back home, much to her mum's annoyance. Mum couldn't see the attraction of staying in a country that didn't really celebrate Christmas 'properly' as she called it and said she had baulked at the price of posting Suzie's present. Suzie noted that her mum's present as a result would not get to her in time, but then again she should really have told Mum sooner that she had no intention of returning to the UK just yet.

Since knowing that her boyfriend had departed her flat yet again she had got Chistine to change the locks and an agency to look after it until she returned. At the moment, there was a young couple that had just moved in to rent it. She figured getting money out of it was better than leaving it empty, but Isabel seemed inexplicably disgruntled about it. Not that it had anything to do with her. Isabel had planned to spend Christmas back in the UK with her 'yet to be met' boyfriend but grumbled that he had 'not managed well' without her. As a result, he'd suddenly 'let go' of his flat without warning.

"How stupid can you be?" Isabel grumbled. "He should have handled it better. Now we have to find somewhere to stay over Christmas. I figure he owes me one, so it had better be the Hilton, or else!"

Even though Isabel was often distant nowadays, Marrakesh without her over Christmas seemed quiet once she'd gone. Suzie spent her time off planning new campaigns for the shop and watching TV. As Tony was staying in Morocco over Christmas and he too was on his own, they decided to join forces and booked into a restaurant for Christmas Day lunch. When the day arrived the meal turned out to be a Marrakesh version of a Sunday dinner, and the two of them lazed happily in the central gardens for the rest of the day. The temperature had been pleasant, but Suzie still got sunburnt.

*

Tony and Suzie waited over the next few weeks for the big explosion to happen following their e-mail to Mr Phipps but it did not arrive. Nothing was said. Sometime later Suzie was allowed to go back to the shop full-time. Perhaps the e-mail had worked, perhaps they could just get on with work now. Perhaps.

Carpet Man was nowhere to be seen and it had been over two months since Suzie had seen him. She hoped he was not unwell and realised for the first time that she had no way of contacting him. However, work at the shop was always 'business as usual' and she was relieved that its location provided some much-needed physical distance from HQ. Andy had been predictably brilliant and was a quiet but faithful support. Even though Suzie had said nothing about what had been going on, he seemed to sense that support was needed.

"Cuppa?" Andy asked.

"I would kill for a cuppa!" Suzie said.

"No need. You have a willing servant here... for a small fee."

"How much? Can I afford it?" Suzie asked, smiling for the first time in months.

"You may have to if you want a cuppa!" Andy grinned.

It was good to be back.

Given the fact that their investigations had put them squarely in the frame, Tony and Suzie pulled back completely. After the two of them had poured over motives for each suspect they had drawn a complete blank and so with no further leads the T&S Detective Agency was disbanded. Neither Suzie nor Tony really wanted to talk about the leak anymore, and having heard nothing from Mr Phipps they just wanted to put the whole thing behind them. Both hoped that that was how the company saw it too, it certainly seemed that way as things steadily improved. As they were both still in their jobs they figured the company server had probably not delivered their e-mail to Mr Phipps that day. They had been ready to 'face the music' and accept whatever happened, but there turned out to be no music to face. The orchestra had gone quiet. Gradually over the next few weeks Tony reported that the sullen silences and staring eyes in the HQ office had grown less, and that he was now left to do his job once more. She was glad for Tony. He was, after all, one of their most dependable employees when all was said and done.

Ding! It was a text from Christine in the UK.

Coming over to see you this weekend, you poor thing. Don't let the *****s grind you down, girl!

Suzie could always rely on Christine to put a smile on her face. Ding! Another text from her.

So… come on… tell me all the latest. What did the 'big boss' say when you sent him the e-mail to get yourself out of trouble?

Suzie hurriedly texted her back and filled her in on what had been happening.

Ding!

How well do you know Tony? He seems to be the one with all the leads, and it sounds like he was alone with Isabel in the boardroom on the day in question.

How could Christine think it was Tony? Suzie texted back:

Well, no… Ahmed was there too, clearing up things when the others had left…

Ding!

Oh… not him then… just making sure.

Suzie texted again.

No. Tony's a good sort. He wouldn't do it. He's one of the most trustworthy people here.

Ding!

Well don't let them grind you down. Stand firm. Bye, hon.

She had a few days to get things ready. A girly weekend was just what the doctor ordered. Suzie marched through the souk to her favourite stallholder on her way back from work that day to gather the veg needed for a wonderful tagine recipe she had found. It would be slow-cooked to produce the smoky flavour they described, and she would cook it on Saturday. That way it would be ready just as Christine got off the plane.

*

Suzie awoke bright and early that Saturday and laid in bed thinking about the weekend ahead. The birds were singing, the sun was shining, and she had not felt like this for some months now. She got up, munched on a croissant, and swigged two cups of coffee on the balcony. Carpet Man was back! He waved to her just as she gulped down the last drop of coffee. *I'll just get my veggies on and then I must say hello to him and Cactus Girl*, she thought. Returning back

149

inside she chopped the veggies and started the tagine off in the oven where it would cook for the next few hours. The airport was on the other side of town and she had decided to walk to shift the last bit of weight she wanted to lose. It had been clinging on for dear life.

"Carpet Man! You're back! Did you have good travels?"

"Always good travels, Berber Girl," he replied.

"So good to see you. It's not the same without you here. I will stop and talk tomorrow because I really want to catch up on your news, but for now I have to get to the airport."

He nodded, smiled his enigmatic smile, and said nothing.

The walk was pleasant. She walked through the central gardens and remembered the day she found that wonderful foundation make-up. The walk also took her past the souk on the other side of town where Tony had first shown her the best places to shop when she first came. She thought about lazing in the shade on Christmas Day. All good memories. Once at the airport she just had time to pick out a small present for Christine at the airport shops and walk over to the arrivals gate where she stood waiting.

"Yoohoo!" Suzie called.

"Hiya, hon! Come here!" Christine hugged her tightly. "What have the beeps been doing to you now? I'll come and beat them up for you. Just point me in the direction of the worst one. I'm ready!"

"You were born ready, Christine! Let's get a taxi and I will tell you all about it." As the two friends shuffled themselves excitedly into a car waiting at the taxi rank,

Suzie began to tell her how everything was returning to normal now.

"About time too," Christine said. "Did they ever get who did it? Who the leak was?"

"No. I think they have their suspicions but they're not saying anything. At least they seem to believe me now, which is the main thing."

Back at the flat Suzie set the table and poured the wine Christine had brought with her. "Thought you may need some *proper* Prosecco," Christine said.

"Here," Suzie replied. "I got you something too." She pushed a small object wrapped in tissue paper towards Christine. It was a camel and Berber figure made out of some kind of metal into a keyring. "To remind you of me in case you ever forget me…"

"As if…"

The tagine was delicious. The lamb was juicy and fruity and was the perfect prelude to the chick flicks they settled down to watch on Netflix. Suzie produced some Turkish delight and the two nibbled away contentedly until teatime.

"So…" Christine started. "Who is this mysterious carpet man I keep hearing about?"

"Did you not see him as we arrived at the flat?"

"Wasn't paying much attention. I was pretty much dying of hunger at the time. Was just thinking about your delicious tagine I was about to eat to notice too much."

"He was the guy at the rug stall."

"Oh. The one with the little girl?"

"Yes. Come on, I will introduce you if you like? Grab your things. I'll show you Moroccan nightlife while I'm at it." Christine changed, had a quick freshen up, and grabbed her purse. But by the time they emerged from the flat door, Carpet Man and Cactus Girl had packed up for the day and had disappeared.

Suzie decided to take Christine to the nearest souk followed by the nearest nightclub that she had been to a few times with work colleagues. It was named 'The Secret Room' and was rumoured to be the most luxurious nightclub in town. It certainly had a trendy vibe and a live band were there tonight. The two bopped away without a care in the world and joined the conga line as it passed. Towards the end of the evening the building's heavens seemed to open and giant multicoloured pieces of confetti rained down on them. Bliss!

The next morning, after a leisurely breakfast of *sfenj*, the two friends went shopping in the souks once again.

"I want to try and buy some of that mint tea we had at breakfast to take back home," Christine said.

"I wouldn't," Suzie said. "They might think you have wacky baccy going through customs." Christine looked dismayed. "Best to buy it direct from their website I reckon." Christine decided to follow Suzie's advice so instead she bought a long-flowing and brightly coloured dress with the money burning in her pocket. After Christine's amusing tales of her hapless Valentine's date last Friday, Suzie was waving her off at the airport all too soon.

On Monday morning Eric sent around an e-mail saying that they would all be glad to know that the leak culprit had been caught some time ago, and since business had returned to normal now all staff at a particular grade could apply for a surprise promotion that was coming up. The post was to be a deputy CEO position. Even Andy had received the e-mail which Suzie supposed was because he had run the shop so well when she had been 'imprisoned' at HQ recently. The phone rang. It was Isabel.

"You going for it, Suzie? The promotion I mean?" she asked.

"Maybe, maybe not." Suzie was not about to tell Isabel, that much she had learnt. "Might do it for the experience, might not. Obviously won't get it with me and Tony being 'suspect number one' recently."

"Have a try," Isabel urged. "They can only say no… You never know. I can't wait. I'm definitely going for it. Youngest female CEO ever, me! Just you wait and see!" Some things didn't change. Life was definitely returning to normal. And about time too.

Chapter 20

Interviews

Isabel and Suzie barely had the chance to talk to each other these days as they had both been so busy, but Suzie suspected that Isabel was inexplicably avoiding her. It was probably all to do with the fact that Eric had been watching hers and Tony's every move and Isabel obviously didn't want to be associated with her.

Suzie put this out of her mind as today she was working on one of the bigger ad campaigns up at HQ. She was now sure that they had been right to send her to Morocco. Suzie had, after all, put the shop back on its feet and today she had created the ad campaign they were running. It was a shame that for a time things had turned unpleasant but that was all over now.

The heat was getting unbearable, which she was told was odd for early March. The throbbing sensation in Suzie's head was tapping out a beat to 'Walkin' back to happiness'. In her mind's eye she pictured a blonde girl with lots of curls in a white cotton dress with brightly coloured geometric patterns on the skirt. She seemed happy enough but surely she was scorching her bare feet as she danced along the flaming-red ground? Delirium was obviously setting in. The heat was affecting everyone's mood in the office and the still air was beginning to fog up Suzie's brain. In fact, the fans had been on at full blast since the air conditioning had packed up last week but they never seemed to make the place any cooler. They just moved the same heavy warm air around. Suzie quickly grasped the pile of papers that were about to take off in the fan's blast and steadied herself.

Eric had announced that any staff member receiving his e-mail and wanting to go for the deputy CEO's job could apply, and all applicants would be certain of an interview as it would be a good learning experience for them. Both her and Isabel had applied plus a couple of others, and today was the day of the interviews. Suzie wondered why Eric had not jumped at the chance to apply seeing as whoever got the job would effectively be his new boss.

Mentally she ran through all of the 'off-shore' contracts HQ had links to as she wanted to show she knew about the whole organisation. All of the contracts without exception seemed to have a problem. There was the new one with a large city supermarket – the boss had left suddenly so that one was on hold. There was the one that only came in last week – no staff were currently available to run the advertising, and the myriad of others that either had money troubles, difficult family politics, or were just hard to handle. She got up and walked towards the lift, her heels clinking noisily along the corridor. "Ah well… here goes nothing."

To her surprise, she saw Carpet Man on the interview panel as she entered the interview room. However, as he was on the co-operative, she guessed he had probably been brought in for local representation. Hopefully he would put in a good word for her, but as this was for experience it probably wouldn't make any difference. There was Eric, Mr Phipps, and a woman from HR that she had never seen before. The interview turned out to be exactly as she expected. Short, functional, and to the point. *Hope they give good feedback*, Suzie thought as she closed the door.

The hour following the interview was filled with action, and Suzie secured three new contracts in one day which was her best ever. The guy came to deliver water for the water-cooler machine, then the air conditioning repair guy came, so the office was now cool as a cucumber for the first time in a week. Equilibrium had returned and Suzie could function properly once again. Isabel stuck her head around the door.

"Just had my interview with the panel, it was a breeze." She wafted her hand and as she did so a large-carat diamond caught the light. "I had them eating out of my hand." Isabel then spent the next twenty minutes telling Suzie how the other poor plebs having interviews would not know what hit them. Suzie would once have been schmoozed by this type of talk and taken it as 'confidence in a job well done'. Now it just came across as 'arrogance based on a complete lack of skills and a web of deceit'. How things had changed.

"Diamond ring, eh, Isabel? Who's the lucky man?"

"Oh, this? I picked this up in the souk, it's a dress

ring," Isabel stated rather too quickly. But Suzie knew a real diamond when she saw it. Isabel usually had the best monthly record for new contracts, but Suzie now questioned how many of these were legit. Isabel flounced out whilst still describing some woefully overpriced pair of shoes that she would buy in celebration of her 'soon to be' new job.

Christine texted her. *Find somewhere private, urgently,* was all it said.

Suzie ran to the loo. She dialled her number. "Christine? You okay?"

"Are you sitting down, Suzie?"

"No but go on. What's the emergency?"

"There's no point beating around the bush. You know some time ago we thought your boyfriend back here may have had a floozie?"

"Yes..." Suzie could hardly bear what was coming next.

"I know who it was... It was Isabel..." All at once Suzie knew it was true. When did it start? Had she actually been seeing him before they came out to Morocco? It would explain why her relationship suddenly went off the boil. She thought she had seen him here in the souks a couple of times. It explained that too. Isabel moving out of their shared Morocco flat... Isabel being distant...

"That treacherous cow!"

"Yes. A friend of mine bumped into your boyfriend and he had no idea she knew me, or you for that matter. He was annoyed with Isabel after forcing him to take her to the Hilton at Christmas. Think it was something about his flat falling through."

"Wait… Isabel told me about that… you mean that it was *my* boyfriend she was talking about?"

"Yes, and that's not the worst of it. They were planning to spend Christmas together in your flat because he had sold his a while before." Suzie was struggling to get her head around this. So he had been lying to her and staying there on and off… with Isabel. And Isabel had been staying there and travelling back to the UK… all without telling her. For the first time it all made sense now.

The cleaner appeared later that day at 3.30pm as usual, but his usual kindly face was frowning. Isabel was nowhere to be seen.

"Miss, I zink you had better see Monsieur Phipp, 'e is asking for you," he said. He looked worried. Mr Phipps was hardly ever mentioned even though, allegedly, he was the owner of the company. He didn't seem to really take much interest in the day-to-day running either. True, he had been on the panel for the interviews which was the first time she had ever seen him since she had arrived in Morocco. Yet, he hadn't even replied to hers and Tony's e-mail before Christmas protesting their innocence. The cleaner seemed to think Mr Phipps calling her back in would be bad news. What could he possibly want with Suzie? Interview feedback?

She stepped out of the office. Eric was now in the corridor to meet her with a serious look on his face. This was not good, certainly nothing trivial. Her heart sank at a rapid rate of knots followed swiftly by her stomach. Surely her interview had not been *that* bad? True, she had missed out a couple of crucial elements that she could have said, but didn't everyone? She was never going to set the world alight but even so… Maybe this had nothing to do with the interview? Maybe this had more to do with the leak? Maybe something Isabel had said. Had she openly blamed Suzie during her interview? It wouldn't be the first time. Suddenly, Suzie then knew what this was about. It was something to do with that grilling she got that day when the suited observer was present. *Oh man*, she thought. She was about to get fired.

"Come into my office and sit down," Eric demanded. This wasn't an invitation, it was a command. He looked at Suzie as if he had just eaten something unpleasant. He motioned towards a vacant chair opposite Mr Phipps.

"Please leave us, Eric," Mr Phipps said. His voice was soft and smooth and sounded younger than the lines on his face would indicate. He had a kind face, lots of laughter lines, but he wasn't laughing right now. Suzie could see Eric was biting back anger as he went out the door, after giving Mr Phipps a curt defamatory bow of the head instead of the deferential one that Suzie expected Eric to use to his boss. He closed the door noisily behind him.

I'm in deep doggie doo-doo, thought Suzie.

"Tell me about yourself." Mr Phipps leaned forward as if he was genuinely interested. It threw Suzie for a moment.

"Well… I am single, I live in the company flat here and have a flat back in the UK. I… er… what do you want to know?" Suzie shrugged. She was at a loss to know what to say.

"Tell me about what you value, your outlook on life. For example, can you walk past a child crying?" This meeting was getting more confusing by the minute. Had someone spotted her walking past an unseen child in the street and complained? Whatever the reason, Isabel must surely be behind this. Seeing the perplexed look on Suzie's face, Mr Phipps then spent the next twenty minutes telling Suzie about the depth of feeling people had here in Morocco about family values. Hadn't Suzie always been respectful to people's ways here? After the long months of politics, the heat, and Isabel's antics, this was more than she could bear. Suzie told him what she thought as she no longer cared what the end result would be. After all, she was about to get fired wasn't she? Isabel was a real 'beep beep' at times. Suzie finished her rant, relieved at the eventual off-loading of all those pent-up frustrations, but her heart was lodged firmly in the pit of her stomach. What a time to say it, they hadn't even told her about the job yet, she should have bitten it back for just a little longer. She had blown all her chances now, and she knew what was coming. It was inevitable. She imagined how painful it would be having to come back to the UK with her tail firmly between her legs. After all the conversations, her hopes, and her dreams. Her Moroccan dreams.

Mr Phipps then threw Suzie for the second time that afternoon. He smiled kindly and said, "You misunderstand. I like your values, and yes, you have always *usually* been respectful." He looked at Suzie with eyes like deep oceans that could swallow you up. Suzie blinked. "I have been observing your performance from afar, and both your line manager and Mr Abdullah have kept me up to date with how you have been doing here. You have the best record for this month's contracts, is that correct?" Suzie blinked again and Mr Phipps took that as a yes. Maybe she would survive this ordeal. A thread of hope? "Tell me, what happened with Mr Kassab all those months ago when you first started... you can be honest." Suzie saw her hope disappear down the plughole, it was clear that Isabel had dumped her in it.

"Mr Kassab was the shopkeeper we went to see on our first task here." Suzie decided not to hold back. What did she have to lose? "I had been waiting for Isabel to arrive for around thirty minutes and I had no idea where she was. This meant that we were late." Suzie explained that she was not making excuses but just recounting the facts, and how she liked to come alongside people and earn their trust, not just expect it. She also said that she never 'bulldozed' people into hard sells like others which were not right for them or their family. That might work in the UK, but not here which is why she was aghast at how Isabel had treated Mr Kassab. Eric had told them to learn the culture here and Suzie did exactly that. Back in the UK it was often expected for you to be a little ruthless, but again, here it was frowned upon. Suzie finished her explanation and Mr Phipps was quiet for a moment. He then explained that Mr Kassab had been very influential in these parts, had put in a complaint, and they had almost lost the shop and its business as a direct result. Suzie had been aware of locals not using the shop for while so she was not surprised to hear this. Her being summoned back to see Mr Phipps was beginning to make more sense now. It was to investigate what actually happened that day. Naturally, Eric had asked Isabel about this event first so Mr Phipps recounted her version of the events to Suzie. Suzie saw a grey mist descending over her future once more, but she found she could not stop. The floodgates opened. She told Mr Phipps respectfully that Isabel had lied her way into Eric's heart but she did not know what to do about this. Suzie said that she had worked hard to turn the shop around to a place where she could grow the company organically through bigger and better ad campaigns. She was no fool and she knew that that was not the usual way for ad agencies to conduct their business but realised that was how it had to be here. She said she believed that the shop should be a place that serves the local people. Mr Phipps was silent. Had Suzie gone too far? He sat with his elbows wide apart on the desk, his fingertips touching each other and his lips. Suzie noticed his gold wedding ring.

After what seemed like forever, he said, "I think I can safely say that I know your thoughts on the matter."

Suzie would have to start clearing her desk tonight. She lowered her eyes. "What about when Eric accused me and Tony of being the leak? Do you now believe we are innocent?"

"Yes," he replied. "Eric had to ask you, and he was sure you had something to do with the leak. You must admit, it was pretty suspicious you and Tony turning up at Treece and Floggs."

"Suspicious yes, but guilty no. It was circumstantial. We had to send you the e-mail that day telling you what had happened. We thought that Eric was the culprit as he meets Jane there, but we drew a blank. Please tell me. Have you found the guilty person yet?"

"I must say I was surprised to receive your e-mail but your story checked out. I understood why you did it and I

162

know that most guilty parties would not think of trying a stunt like that, they would just lie low. It rather convinced me you were being framed. Eric's reason for being there is simple: Jane is his new partner. He just didn't want people to know as he thought that might put him in the frame, and it would have done. However, given Eric's compromised position regarding his relationship with this woman and his errors of judgement concerning Isabel, I asked him not to apply for the deputy CEO role."

Suzie exhaled slowly. She felt overwhelmed with this new piece of knowledge and would tell Tony as soon as she left here. "I had no idea... I guess that explains the phone calls he made and why Jane told him we had visited there... *And* the roasting we then got from him." So, Eric was innocent after all. Nasty, but innocent.

"We decided instead to allow things to get back to normal to allow the culprit to feel that they had got away with it, but meanwhile we laid traps... And that is how we found that Isabel was not as innocent as she was making out."

So they really did think Isabel was guilty! Suzie wondered how much proof they had.

"I have made a decision," Mr Phipps announced. He extended a brown hand towards Suzie, grasped her hand in his, and shook it vigorously. "Congratulations!"

"Sorry?" Suzie blinked.

"You have been successful in your interview. We are offering you the job."

"What?"

"You have the job here. Permanently. That is, if you want it?"

"Was this an interview?"

He smiled a warm smile. "Forgive me, I was fairly certain you were right for the job after your panel interview, and the feedback given to me thereafter from certain parties, but I wanted to make sure for myself. You see, a lot rides on getting this right. Me telling you about family values here was not the sermon you supposed. It was me confirming to you that you are perfect for the job."

"Oh."

"Me asking you about Mr Kassab when you first came was also not the 'dressing down' you supposed either."

"Ah… apologies." Suzie blushed. "I was certain Isabel would get the job."

"What Isabel fails to notice is that kindness goes a long way out here and unkindness takes a long time to be forgotten. You, my dear, are naturally kind." He continued, "I have been concerned with Isabel's performance for a while, and so was the UK branch."

Not for the first time Suzie's mouth fell open.

"Alarm bells are also now ringing over the way she dealt with Mr Kassab. Which incidentally, she blamed you for. She would no doubt do well in some UK companies as she is so self-assured, but a more sensitive approach is needed here. We decided to send her here to see if better customer relations would rub off on her, but there is clearly no evidence of that. As I said, I have also been keeping track of your performance too. I am not the distant figure that some believe, my decisions feed into all of the daily decisions you see here. Isabel is not right for Morocco and I intend to do something about that, not that your line manager approves of my decisions. I have been working from home whilst my wife has been seriously ill, but now that she is better I will be coming into the office much more from now on. Eric didn't seem to be too happy about that decision either." He smiled at Suzie aware that she was sitting in stunned silence. "You can close your mouth again now."

"Sorry!" Obediently Suzie closed her mouth. Her heart had seared a hole in her stomach and was now sitting round about her feet. How stupid must she have seemed to Mr Phipps.

"Join me for a drink, we have much to talk about." He pressed the intercom and asked Sally to bring in a tray of coffee, mint tea and biscuits. Suzie wondered where Eric was; he would be livid that they were still in his office and he had been 'shooed' out. Gradually, Suzie began to relax as they talked, and she earnestly discussed business, interspersed with more apologies. It was clear that Mr Phipps had obviously decided to put her outburst down to the heat and passion about her job (thank God). He explained how hard it can be to receive the proper recognition in the UK when account managers, being the client-facing side of things, often took the credit for all the hard work from creative people like her. As such, they had decided to put Suzie in the failing print shop to see how far she could fly when given a real chance, as the UK situation didn't really allow for that kind of growth. He went onto say that given the fact it was all but dead it would not have mattered if Suzie failed but she had instead surpassed their expectations. Not only had she put the shop back on its feet but it now had dependable staff, a high level of contract sales, and was running ad campaigns all on its own. Back in the UK they had noticed that Isabel was great in the boardroom but tended to put customer's backs up. They therefore thought that Morocco, being the respectful family-orientated place that it was, may teach her better client relations. Isabel had been placed at HQ so that they could keep an eye on her. "You would be forgiven if you thought that Isabel had got the better deal being placed at HQ. Little did we think that she was capable of the deviant behaviour that has just come to light though," he finished.

"Deviant behaviour?" Suzie asked.

"Already I have said too much. This must *not* go beyond this room as some do not wish me to tell you, because they still suspect you. Even now we do not know the full extent of what Isabel has been doing, but we know she is involved. Suzie, the inquisition we put you through in Eric's office that day was necessary to see if you were a willing and knowing participant, because we knew you two were friends. We suspected Isabel was embezzling from client accounts but could not prove it until now."

"I knew it!" she exclaimed under her breath. Oh wow! So that explained the right royal roasting Suzie had received, and the general 'strained atmosphere' she had felt at HQ on previous occasions. It also explained why Isabel had been more distant recently.

"We knew you could not have been the person using other people's logins to get at the client accounts in question, as they were accessed at HQ computers at times you were not here, but it was possible that you could have been in collusion with Isabel."

"As you know, I definitely was not. But can I ask something, Mr Phipps?"

"Yes, of course."

"Everything seemed to go silent over the leak. Do we know who did it yet?"

Mr Phipps stopped for a second and looked at Suzie. "Now is not the time to go into that, but I have another confession. I told you that we placed you at the shop to see if you could fly. What I haven't told you is that Mr Abdullah, your 'carpet man', was asked to mentor you to see if you would learn Moroccan ways. He reports that you were a most willing apprentice."

"Oh!" Suzie exhaled noisily with her hand placed over her mouth. "You mean… it was all… did I? Oh… I mean…"

"Yes," Mr Phipps interrupted. "I hope you forgive me? It was necessary that you didn't know so that I could see what you were truly made of."

"So… all that time… Meeting Mr Abdullah was not a chance meeting?"

"No, I'm afraid it was planned," he said with a warm smile. "Although Eric was unaware of this plan. It was solely my doing." Mr Phipps continued, "Carpets don't sell well outside your flat but Mr Abdullah was prepared to take the hit. We had to make your meeting with him feel natural and you did very well. You made the shop a success when we could have lost it and you are well-liked. You have succeeded where mostly men do the business, you treat older clients with respect, you are much more confident now, and your manner engenders trust. By the way, we gave the same chance to Isabel initially but she did not take kindly to Mr Abdullah's help." Suzie could just picture Carpet Man trying to give her the benefit of his wisdom and her telling him to 'go take a hike'. She had never had time for local niceties which had 'passed her by' altogether. Mr Phipps eyed her attire as he got up. "You will, however, need to buy yourself a few smarter suits…" he said as he opened Eric's door for them to leave "…as you will not be taken seriously as a senior manager without them. But I must say, I was not fully aware of all of your skills before today's interview so we will need to revise your salary, it's not nearly enough. If you still want the job, of course?"

'Oh, yes. Definitely!' Suzie cried.

What had just happened here? She walked back to the office and readied herself to go home. She sat for a few minutes at her desk in a semi-stupor. Isabel was still nowhere to be seen, maybe she had been told that Suzie had been 'summoned' and out of guilt scarpered, just in case? She had probably gone home as it was after work hours now and she never stopped late if she could help it. Maybe she had got wind of the company being onto her now? Had she really been embezzling? And… Wow! Suzie had actually been given one of the most prestigious jobs going. She could hardly believe it all!

Chapter 21

The Tide Has Turned

Suzie no longer had the usual compulsion to tell mum her news, but she thought she should at least mention what had happened. She readied herself for the quips about 'how her success at the interviews must be attributed to Isabel' and picked up the phone.

"Hi, Mum," Suzie started. "They were running promotion interviews for our grade recently and guess what? I got the job. I'll be deputy CEO soon..." Suzie waited for the putdown, but for once it didn't come. Instead, Mum just asked a few questions about the role and what she would be doing. Were all mums this unpredictable?

*

The next day Suzie expected to see Isabel stroll in late as usual, gather her entourage around her over coffee, and make a leisurely start to the day. But there was no Isabel and what's more, no Eric. Midday came and went and still no sign of either of them. A chance meeting with Harry shed some light. Apparently after Suzie had gone back to her HQ desk and left for the day yesterday, Mr Phipps had summoned Eric to his office. Harry and a few others had stayed late to finish their work on a project with a tight deadline and they had heard Eric yelling at the top of his voice at Mr Phipps. Eric had told him point by point why Suzie was so completely wrong for the deputy CEO job and how it should be Isabel instead. Mr Phipps had then responded in kind and outlined point by point why he was sending both Isabel and Eric back to work in the UK, how Isabel would be reprimanded and put on performance management. He had told Eric how Suzie had been 'much maligned by both of them', and it had to stop. Mr Phipps then said he would now be more 'hands on' at the office from now on as things 'were slipping' under Eric's control.

"You'll like this next bit," Harry said. "The few that were left here all heard the row going on because it was so loud you couldn't miss it. Mr Phipps told Eric that Isabel was a blunt instrument, always late, unprofessional, and lazy… the list was endless. He told Eric how Isabel had blamed you for all her many failings and how Eric would 'have to get his act together' and treat you with respect for the remaining time he had in Morocco." Harry blushed. "Personally, I couldn't believe what a cow Isabel had been to you, so I poured coffee all over her prized Gucci leather handbag that she always leaves on her seat…"

"You didn't!" Suzie laughed.

"I certainly did! I should have put squirty cream on

it too. That's nothing to what she had obviously put you through. Serves her right. I'm sorry. I believed the rumours that you and Tony had done something wrong." Harry went on to explain how Isabel had then been summoned into Mr Phipps' office.

"I thought Isabel had scarpered. So... she was still here? What did he say to her?"

"Don't know as there was no shouting," he said. "But she later came out of the office with her head down and face like thunder. She went straight home without a word."

*

As they were all supposed to be working on a massive ad campaign, Suzie was up at HQ for the rest of the week. She kept looking for Isabel but she was nowhere to be seen. During coffee time with Mr Phipps it transpired that he had told Isabel to spend the rest of the week thinking seriously about her future and the move back to the UK. He told Suzie that he had been lenient and had secretly planned to have a police escort waiting at Heathrow Airport as her welcome party, as the penalty for stealing large sums of money here was very harsh. However, somehow Isabel must have got wind of this and had cried off sick for her remaining week in Morocco.

"Do you know anything about the leak, Suzie? I have to ask," he said.

"Absolutely not. It definitely wasn't me," said Suzie. "In fact, I would like to know who did it."

Mr Phipps continued. Isabel had not apologised, not bothered to hand in her notice, and not even come back to the office to pick up her things. Consequently, Mr Phipps said he had sacked her.

"Isabel didn't even bother to say goodbye to me," Suzie said.

Mr Phipps nodded. "Probably for the best."

*

Today, Eric's lip was curling like an angry dog subdued by its owner. He had obviously been told to 'be quiet' by Mr Phipps but he was nevertheless intent on expressing his suppressed agitation at the situation. He made sure Suzie knew how unhappy he was about it all. Under normal circumstances, Suzie would have been slightly intimidated by this but instead a blissful joy kept bubbling up inside her. He would soon no longer be her line manager, and her future was about to get substantially better. For some reason her thoughts kept getting interrupted by straplines and idioms: 'This is the first day of the rest of your life'. Suzie could not stop the smile creeping over her lips which did nothing to help Eric's mood. 'Carpe diem, seize the day' – Suzie would make sure that Mr Phipps had chosen her well. She thought of Mum back in the UK and the agency looking after her flat. She would have to sell it now as she had definitely decided to stay in Morocco. She considered how far she had come in just twelve months: she was more relaxed, confident in her own abilities, and had learnt how to sell and negotiate well for new contracts. She even looked the part now – sleek hair, great make-up – she was no longer the 'weighty girl' she had once been. Furthermore, she was no longer held captive by Isabel's treachery, her family's negativity, and her boyfriend's indifferent unfaithfulness. She had become the person she had always longed to be.

The atmosphere in the UK HQ had been totally different to the central HQ here in Morocco. In the UK, it was like a hotbed. The constant pressure to perform at the UK HQ at the top level was immense and the result was usually one of two: you either had the agency impressed deeply into you like a branding iron (and your career took off), or you were consumed by its intense heat. You either became strong and confident, or you left suffering and defeated. If you didn't keep up you were left by the wayside like a piece of discarded litter. There were no half measures. It couldn't have been more different to the values here.

She had often noted that people came and went at the Moroccan HQ and had assumed that this was because the job was so fast-paced and dynamic. It was not for everyone. Rumours of violent personality clashes, complete breakdowns, and potential mutiny bubbling under the surface at the Moroccan HQ had reached Suzie's ears and via Isabel. At the time she had believed them. She now realised these rumours were untrue and just Isabel trying to make her own job sound more exciting. She also realised that the company often used HQ here as a training ground for up-and-coming employees, just like they had done for her and Isabel. The only thing that usually remained the same were the core staff, and she was now one of them. Yes, this Moroccan HQ was less of a 'bubbling mutiny' and more like a 'fermenting ground'. There was always something of interest going on, things were always changing, and there was always something new to take on board. For better or worse, the environment seemed to force fledglings to 'cut their wings early' which some loved, and some hated. You either sank or swam. Fortunately, Suzie had had enough experience when she arrived here for this not to bother her too much but she too had been changed. Suzie considered whether Isabel had been the necessary 'agitation' for her to bloom (like yeast agitates bread when mixed with warm liquids) but no, that would be giving Isabel far too much credit. The 'friendship' had been turbulent and even volatile at times. It was true that a very tiny bit of her own vigorous growth could have been due to Isabel at times, but she certainly owed much more to the carpet man then she ever would to Isabel. He had always been ready to share his infinite wisdom and people like him inspire others to do something much greater than they could imagine. Suzie had learnt a great deal from him and from what some described as his 'prosaic ramblings'. It had generated a force to be reckoned with within her and she owed him so much.

Her physical transformation from 'porky pig lady' to 'deputy CEO' was due to the fabulous discovery of mineral foundation and her wonderful 'Swedish chef' hair stylist, Antonio. What a great find he was! Most hairdressers ask what you want in terms of style or hair length and then do what they think, not what you've asked for. But he did what you asked for and talked of 'movement in the hair'. He would then cut to enhance the natural wave of the hair and the result was truly wonderful each time. A well-kept appearance and well-cut clothes really did make a difference in meetings with local businessmen as they took what Suzie said seriously, just as Mr Phipps had said.

Her experience here had transformed her into a stronger person. Yes, the Moroccan HQ was a fermenting ground. The design of the building made you feel like you were working in an impressive greenhouse. When people's careers were placed in this greenhouse, the environment forced career 'seedlings' to sprout. Suzie stopped her train of thought for a second to consider Isabel. If she was going to follow the analogy, Isabel's 'seedling' had become pest-ridden and had infected other seedlings.

When they had first arrived the ambient surroundings had seduced Suzie into believing that Isabel got the better deal. However, she now knew she had actually been much better off at the shop. As her employer had thought the shop was all but lost, she had been allowed to be more or less to be her own boss. Suzie learnt that the Moroccan HQ had historically either ignored Suzie's shop (believing it to be inconsequential) or treated it like a bit of a hot potato depending on what was going on at the time. This had still been the case when she had arrived, which had meant that she had been left to run the shop without too much interference from above. This had worked in her favour and had allowed her to impress them unhindered. What's more, the lack of constant supply of wonderful cake at the shop had definitely had an impact on Suzie's waistline. She thought back to the time when she was waiting in the café for Isabel just before they entered the Moroccan TV business show. That version of herself was flustered, red-faced, and had no dress sense whatsoever. She realised now she had been unconfident but never really been able to put that into words until now.

"Who is this young gazelle we have here?" a male voice broke into her thoughts. It was Andy the photographer.

"Gazelle? You gotta be joking."

"Sleek hair, long legs? Counts as a gazelle in my book," he said, grinning his usual cheeky smile. "So what's the line up for today, boss lady?" Their two heads bent over the daily planning sheet and they fell into deep discussion.

*

Carpet Man encouraged Suzie to celebrate soon after she had received news of her promotion. He had insisted on inviting her to his home to meet his family. She thought that family values were important to him so she had accepted.

His lounge was almost entirely surrounded on each wall with banquettes covered in tapestries and cushions. The benches looked hard but were surprisingly comfortable. A large Persian-looking rug filled the floor space in the middle of the room where more cushions were piled for his grandchildren to play on. To Suzie's surprise, the cactus girl and her sister were there too. The carpet man said he had more or less adopted them. "Come, I want you to meet Eric's replacement, but don't say I told you yet." He winked. Suzie followed him obediently into the food-preparation area. There, in an impeccable English suit was a younger version of the carpet man. "This is Aksil, my son. Son, this is Suzie, your new boss."

"Pleased to meet you." Suzie breathed. She felt the same whoosh of adrenaline that she had felt the first time she met the carpet man, but this guy was way more handsome and a similar same age as her. He had the same faraway look in his eyes that all Berbers seemed to have and Carpet Man's enigmatic smile. His eyes were hazel just like his dad's, but there were also flecks of olive green.

"It means 'strength and speed' or 'cheetah' in some dialects," Aksil said. "My name, that is."

"I have no idea what my name means." Suzie laughed. "Probably 'she'll make it one day' or something like that." Oops. That was inappropriate joking like that as she was soon to be his boss. She was also supposed to impress him with her professional distance.

"Graceful lily," he said. "Your name means graceful lily."

Suzie blushed. "I like that," she said. Having just met him she didn't want to ask how he knew. She hated herself for blushing too. It was not professional.

Aksil looked over to where the food was now being dished out. "I believe the meal is ready," he said. Aksil beamed at Suzie and she beamed back. Carpet Man noticed the way they looked at each other. A smile spread across his face and his eyes twinkled as he poured out drinks for everyone. "Cheers, as you English like to say. Congratulations, Suzie, my honorary Berber girl, and congratulations, Aksil. Cheers everyone." They all raised their glasses and made their way to the table. New country, new life and now new job. Suzie could not be happier. She had fulfilled her Moroccan dream. Away from her negative family she had been free to be herself for the first time in her life. Aksil put his hand on hers as they talked. Suzie would have to be careful working with this really handsome guy. Very careful indeed...

A month or two later, with Easter well and truly gone, Suzie received an envelope addressed to her. Inside was a small photograph of Isabel in a smart Chanel two-piece. She was draped elegantly on an expensive yacht, champagne in hand. No letter, and no note of explanation. Just a smug smile on her face. Suzie supposed this was Isabel's way of saying that she was 'still in the land of the living' and 'living it large'. *Yeah, right!* Suzie determined in her heart that she would nail Isabel one day as she was sure in her heart of hearts that she was the cause of the leak somehow. Perhaps Mr Phipps would confide in her more now that she would be working closely with him… but enough of that for now. Suzie no longer felt any irritation or pity for Isabel, she no longer cared. She dropped the photograph into the wastepaper bin and closed the door behind her.

Acknowledgements

My thanks goes to my loving husband, who did the first proofread of the book and painted the picture of Carpet Man for the back page.

Thanks to Ali Pardoe, who gave me her comments on my plot and proofread for punctuation and typographical errors.

Thanks to all the Royston Writers Circle, who have encouraged me in my writing.

Thanks to the 'Lichfield lot' and all those who have listened and given me feedback when developing my characters.

If this book has inspired you to pursue your own dreams in Morocco, here are few words you may need to get started!

ENGLISH	MOROCCAN ARABIC	FRENCH
Hello	Ahlan	Bonjour
Goodbye	Ma'a ElSalama	Au revoir
See you soon	Wada'an	A bientôt
Please	Min Fadilak	S'il vous plait
Thanks	Shokran	Merci
Yes	Na'am	Oui
No	Laa	Non
Where is my camel?	?ayn jamli	Ou est mon chameau?

If you enjoyed *Moroccan Dreams*, you may also enjoy
Part Two in Davina Calbraith's next book:

Moroccan Liaisons: Marrakesh or bust!

Suzie (28) has her dream job with her dream boss at
the advertising agency HQ. She is a girl who has it all…
almost. Now she longs to find the man of her dreams. With
her stylish appearance and new-found confidence, Suzie
realises that she has more choice than she thinks. She has
attracted the attention of one admirer in particular and
things could not be better…

…But life has a way of surprising you.

Thinking that she has freed herself from the
manipulative clutches of Isabel (her former best friend),
Suzie is shocked when Interpol come to visit. As her love
life blossoms, a tangle of secrets and lies keep leading their
way back to Isabel's crimes. Will they catch her? And has
Suzie seen the last of Isabel? Can the ad agency and print
shop survive the bad press?